THE MAD EMPEROR

THE MAD EMPEROR

The DoomSayer Journeys Book 3

STEVE WETHERELL

"There will come a time when the world will stand united in fear of the inevitable, in awe of the unknown. They will wail as one, united in lamentation at the end of all things. And at this time, I will be there to proclaim, indeed with much satisfaction, that I bloody well told them so, didn't I?"

-From the chronicles of Celia Doom

Preface

Where to begin?

We've seen the nuclear waste of a feckless world bundled and rocketed into space, oblivious to its final destination.

We've seen a starship crash, its well-meaning crew stranded on the world they were supposed to watch over, their message of warning never received.

We've seen the young volunteer, venturing out from his isolated community into a wide, hostile world.

We didn't see a funeral. A mourning city lamenting the passing of their queen. An emperor standing indifferently, his thoughts elsewhere while the coffin was lowered into the earth. We didn't see a duke, his face ashen. We didn't see a princess, her eyes red-raw with grief.

We didn't see the emperor walk as if in a dream around his study, listening to the faint whisperings that only he could hear.

We didn't see the astronomers, looking up at the new star in their sky and coming to some very worrying conclusions indeed.

Where to begin?

Mr. Random floated in the void, the fledgling star the only source of light for endless miles around. He floated and drummed his long fingers idly on his knees.

Random was a man who was not really a man. He was an avatar for forces both powerful and malignant, forces that would rather see oblivion than what they perceived as disorder. And so, this agent of deconstruction sat patiently in space, his mind on his mission. He waited in the void. After a while, he began to sing to himself, a calming nonsense ditty. Though, of course, in space, no one can hear you sing.

A flock of faint, wavering shapes began to congregate at the edge of his perception. They had arrived. The bloated, whale-like race Mr. Random had been tracking for eons. They were here.

They towed with them a block of hyper-dense matter, unfathomable in its hugeness. Random could not see the means by which they moved such a payload, but he had given up trying to understand the aliens a long time ago. They were advanced—scarily advanced. Trying to communicate with them was like an ant trying to communicate with the sun.

Random watched as they began their strange dance, space/time becoming fluid and unstable around them. They were building again, warping the space around them in their inimitable manner. Mr. Random grinned. It would likely be millennia before what they were building began to take shape. But he could wait. Oh yes, he could wait…

Operation Deadwaker

Mernin Cobonon, Grand Tutor of the Enlightened Researchers, Argustin Division, wiped his high brow with a lace handkerchief. He wasn't, he felt, cut out for the Bone Desert sun. Nor, he felt, was he cut out for archaeology as an *active* career—that is to say, the parts of archaeology that involved going outside.

Oh, he was very good at looking through ancient texts and could talk for hours on the marital rites of the Bean People of Faburtar (you couldn't very well become Grand Tutor without being able to bore even the most enthusiastic of students to tears), but the actual *practical* aspect of archaeology he had always left to the students and lesser faculty members. But now, with the personal attention of the Emperor focused squarely on his department, Mernin had been forced to take a more hands-on role in the proceedings of Operation Deadwaker.

Not that he could really contribute much to the process—the annoyingly enthusiastic students supported by cheap Nastren labor were making very good progress—but Mernin had to be seen to be making an effort, lest he draw even more personal attention from the Emperor.

He looked up at the huge, stone pyramid erupting from the sand like an arrowhead piercing the earth.

It was one of the hundreds of ancient Nastren tombs that were the final resting places of long-dead kings and queens, but this one was slightly different. The hieroglyphics, those markings that normally told in overelaborate ways of how fantastic such-and-such a long-forgotten ruler had been, were completely different from any Mernin had previously encountered. This worried him. He had studied Nastren tombs throughout his career, had written the definitive work on the subject, and he could find absolutely no similarities between these hieroglyphics and the countless others he had seen.

He remembered Emperor Draegul's vague and impossible-sounding orders to locate and explore every single pyramid in the Bone Desert and to report when he found something out of the ordinary. Thus, Operation Deadwaker, the biggest exhumation in history, had begun. That had been fifteen years ago. Now they had found this new tomb, with its indecipherable markings and its unusually smooth stone...

Mernin had reported the findings to Draegul, of course, but the orders had remained unchanged—to enter and explore the pyramid. Mernin was not looking forward to doing so. He had read enough about ancient Nastren curses—and seen first-hand some of the deadly traps used to guard the tombs—to be extra-cautious about tomb-raiding. This new pyramid, though, seemed to radiate an aura of menace he had never experienced before. Even as he lay down in his tent to sleep at night, he could swear he heard a faint and constant humming noise, like the calling of trapped souls.

Mernin shivered despite the desert heat, then nearly jumped out of his skin when someone shouted his name. He turned to see the familiar and irritatingly eager face of Jimar, his personal assistant, whose half-naked body was equal parts glistening with sweat and matte with dust.

"Grand Tutor! Grand Tutor!" he called excitedly.

"Slow down, boy," huffed Mernin. "You're liable to collapse, running around like that in this accursed sun. Now what is it?"

"The entrance! I'm sure I've found the entrance!"

Despite his bad mood, Mernin couldn't suppress the leap of excitement in his heart. "Where? How? Where?"

Jimar said nothing, but ran off into the distance, motioning for Mernin to follow.

"Wait! Wait for me!" cried the older man, breaking into a half-jog.

Eventually, huffing and blowing, Mernin caught up with his apprentice and was amazed to see that, a furlong or so from the pyramid proper, a small tomb had been unearthed. Four plain and unadorned walls of stone erupted from the sand, climbing to a slightly triangular roof.

"When was this discovered?" demanded Mernin.

"Just this morning," said Jimar. "I'm sure it's the entrance!"

The older man looked at the tomb, then at the massive pyramid. "How can you be sure?" he said. "It looks like an external tomb to me. Nowhere near the pyramid base."

"That's the thing, sir," said Jimar, his voice shaking with excitement. "We've been doing some more sonar readings. It looks as though this isn't the base at all!"

Mernin frowned and looked up at the pyramid. It was already massive by the standards of the other tombs, and he had been sure that they had finally located the base. "You're sure?" he asked.

"Yes, sir," Jimar continued. "It's been said that the base continues down—and not just a little, sir, but for miles! Can you imagine? The pyramid continues down for *miles*!"

Mernin gulped. Draegul would have to hear about this, but for now, one thing was bothering him greatly. "Jimar, how did you know to look for the entrance here?" he said.

Jimar looked blank for a moment. "It will sound silly, sir," he said reproachfully.

"Try me," Mernin replied.

"It came to me in a dream, sir," said Jimar. "I swear, it was as though someone was whispering in my ear while I slept."

Mernin said nothing and tried to suppress the cold shudder that ran down his spine. "Get it open," he said, and made his way back to his tent. Once there, he opened a large bottle of brandy.

Somewhere on the edge of hearing, a faint humming was coming from deep below them. He drank a shot of the sweet brandy in a single gulp. Jimar's discovery had put them weeks ahead of schedule, but he wondered whether the younger man would be so enthusiastic when it came to venturing down into the darkness of the pyramid, and what would be down there waiting for him when he did.

HANDEN, Xharon, Azron, and Bip rode with little pause, their steeds keeping a steady pace across the ever-lusher landscapes. They did so for a day and half, spurred on by the sense of urgency that came from knowing that the new star in the sky, as pretty as it looked, was the first clue to an approaching astral disaster.

The plains around the Oaken Mons were wide and rolling. Cusps of trees and woods were spaced far enough apart that the landscape was largely uninterrupted, sporting only long, green grass as far as the eye could see. It was a world away from the comparatively lifeless Dozantyne Shrub, with sudden bursts of rain that would freshen the ground, making it erupt with a smell of sheer vitality that Bip had never experienced.

As they rode, Bip kept one eye on the skies, charting the progress of the star. It hung there, slightly foggy in the daytime sky, a ghost of things to come. At night, it shone a brilliant silver, as though a cluster of stars had got together to form a gang, hanging around outside some interstellar off-license.

It was getting bigger, too. Not so much that a casual observer would notice, but for Bip, who looked up at the sky every other minute, the light was becoming slightly but maddeningly larger. For a day and half there had been nothing to distract Bip from the glare of the new light in the sky. The sensation of knowing that your imminent doom was hovering just above the horizon was an unsettling one. It was like someone constantly staring hard at the back of your neck.

Finally, they reached Argustin, the capital of the Empire, their final destination. From a distance, the city seemed to sprawl across hills and valleys like a static ocean of stone, glass, and steel. Towers pointed rudely at the sky, and domes and the ornate turrets of elevated mansions broke the surface of the rooftops here and there like huge, expensive bubbles. Largest and grandest of them all stood the glowing crystalline bulk of Dawncastle, resplendent and hypnotic as it cycled through every hue of the setting sun. Against the early evening skies, the city of Argustin twinkled and winked and hinted at money.

Except, of course, for the industrial quarter to the west of the capital, where the city suddenly clung low and paranoid, an artificial turf of long, flat roofs, extruding chimneys like cheap cigarettes, all puffing a soft brown fog into the permanent haze that floated over the quarter like a lonely ghost. This was where the doomsayers traveled.

"Somehow I imagined the crown of the Empire would be a little more showy," remarked Azron as they approached the rusted arches of the industrial quarter's main entrance.

"If we'd gone around to the front gates, you'd have been welcomed with sky-high fountains of the purest mineral water and triumphant golden arches etched with the names and stories of a thousand heroes," said Xharon, airily.

"So why didn't we go 'round that way, then?"

"Because you would also have been welcomed by many guards with many triumphant, golden, and *very sharp* axes."

"Ah."

They passed under the rusted archway. A man sat slouched in the guardhouse, reading a newspaper. He looked up at the travelers with tired eyes, then turned back to his reading.

"Besides," continued Xharon, "this is where my father lives."

Azron and Bip exchange a glance.

"Sorry if I'm being a bit simple," said Azron, "but didn't you say you were a princess?"

"Yes?"

"Well, this just doesn't seem like a very...*princessy* place to grow up."

"Oh, no," laughed Xharon. "I never lived here. My father's an industrialist and an inventor—he works here. Hardly ever spends any time up at the mansion."

At the mention of the word "mansion," the doubt left Azron's eyes, and a familiar calculating grin spread across his face.

Handen wasn't really paying attention to the conversation of his traveling companions. As was his habit, he was scrutinizing his new environment, assessing the terrain with an expert eye, taking note of possible escape routes and public mood. The Industrial Quarter was a slightly intimidating place. The buildings were uniformly gray and ordered, each road and turning angled almost exactly the same. The streets were all numbered rather than named—they were currently riding down A26 with turnings onto B5 and B5A. Even the people they rode past, few and far between, looked similar to one another, all dressed in identical denim boiler-suits and flat caps, with identical streaks of grime obscuring their features. They hurried from one place to another, eyes downcast, identical expressions of weariness on their faces. No one seemed to take any notice of the travelers.

"It seems a bit deserted," said Bip.

Almost as soon as he had said this, a shrill whistle sounded from a nearby building. Dozens of others whistling erupted in response, echoing from various distant corners of the Industrial Quarter. Before the initial shock of the sudden noise had faded, doors banged open in every building on the road, and the boiler-suited men flocked out in the thousands, grumbling and laughing and marching with military precision to their respective homes. For a moment, it was if an ocean of denim had suddenly flooded the dusty streets, and then, just as suddenly, it was over. The last of the workers rounded the corners, and all that was left was the sound of fading footsteps.

"That was odd," said Bip.

"Clocking-off time," explained Xharon. "They've all gone to get their dinner before the night shift starts."

"They work nights as well as days?" said Bip. "They must have plenty of money."

"Oh, good grief, no," said Xharon. She squinted her eyes as if remembering a well-taught lesson. "If you pay them too much, they won't work as hard or as long. Common knowledge. If you keep them at a low wage, they'll work longer hours. It's good labor management."

"Is it?" said Handen, raising an eyebrow. "Has anyone asked their opinion?" He gestured to the retreating backs of the workers.

Xharon looked momentarily confused. "Of course not," she said. "They're not in charge, are they?"

Handen looked blankly at the princess and spurred his horse forward.

Bip could hear Azron muttering as the horse trotted away. "You see, that's why I just steal stuff. Everybody's happier all 'round."

Xharon's brow furrowed in confusion. "Was it something I said?"

Bip shrugged. "Where I come from, you work until the job's done and get a share of the rewards. I don't know much about labor management."

"How strange," said Xharon, and urged her horse into a trot.

THEY ARRIVED at the factory on C12. It had no name and was referred to only as "the factory on C12." It was identical to every other factory they had passed—huge, gray, rectangular, and drastically soulless. In the increasing darkness of nightfall, lit by the inadequate flush of the gas lamps, there was something slightly nightmarish about the massive metal boxes. Bip shivered, then jumped as Xharon suddenly pounded on the huge wooden doors again, the tortured hinges screeching a metallic wail through the still night air.

"Daddy? Daddy, it's me, Xharon! Open the door, please!"

"*Daddy?*" muttered Azron. Handen nudged him in the ribs.

For a moment, the only sound was the hum and whir of distant machinery.

"Are you sure he'll be here? Maybe he went home for dinner," said Bip.

Xharon shook her head. "Daddy doesn't know the meaning of the words clocking off. He wouldn't eat or sleep at all if there wasn't someone employed to remind him to."

Bip and Azron exchanged a look that was becoming a common reaction to one of Xharon's comments, then started suddenly at the sound of heavy bolts shifting.

The door creaked open to reveal a dozen shining eyes. Bip found himself hesitantly stepping backward, perfectly flanked by Azron and Handen.

Then came a voice. "My word, Xharon, what on Bersch are you doing out in the cold in your underpants?"

There was an embarrassed silence, and Xharon shifted uncomfortably in her over-simplified leather outfit, her face suddenly turning as red as her hair. A short, round man emerged from behind the door holding an open coat. The shining eyes revealed themselves to be the multifarious lenses of a bizarre pair of adjustable spectacles, the dozens of distorted glass discs magnifying the old man's balding head, each in a different way. He wore a shirt and trousers that looked as if they had never been ironed and held the ensemble together with a bright red bow tie that drooped miserably over his collar. He threw a coat, a tweed jacket with leather patches, over Xharon in a thoughtful but ineffectual attempt at modesty.

"What have I told you about walking about in your smalls? People will think you've gone quite, quite mad! It won't do, it really won't!" The man's voice was musically clear but couldn't seem to settle on a single pitch for too long, like a jazz flute player who has had one inspirational cigarette too many.

Xharon struggled out of the coat. "*Daddy*, how many times? This is perfectly normal attire for a warrior princess!" she whined.

"Such nonsense! Such nonsense! Of all the nonsense I ever did have the misfortune to bear, this, by far, is the most nonsensical!" The man suddenly froze in his flustering and turned slowly toward Bip. "And who, by all that is embarrassingly unexpected, are you?"

Xharon, shrugging the coat away from her shoulders, let out a theatrical sigh. "These are my *friends*, Daddy."

The old man blinked for a while, then made an effort to pat down the erratic cotton-wool tufts of his white hair. "Friends, eh?" he said and began to look the men up and down, adjusting the lenses on his glasses as he scrutinized each in turn before shaking their hands with mad enthusiasm. "Always good to meet friends of Xharon's. I'm her father, you know. The name's Riley—*Professor* Riley DeChambre. She doesn't bring many people to see me, you know. Probably thinks I'm an embarrassment—I said an *embarrassment*, if you can imagine, coming from a girl who walks around in her knickers. An *embarrassment!* Come in, come in, come in, do—have some tea, please, follow me, come in!" And then the man was gone, back through the door before anyone else had a chance to speak.

Xharon shrugged. "That's my father," she said.

Bip turned to Azron and Handen in turn. Both merely mirrored Xharon's shrug. They entered the factory.

2

An Appointment with Doom

If Bip had thought the factories nightmarish from the outside, the inside was the twisted aberration of a dreaming madman. Not since his brief time in the Dome had Bip seen so much metal in one place, though here, rather than the smooth, almost infinite walls of the ancient spacecraft, the factory was littered with massive contraptions that hulked like rusted monoliths. Glasswork of intricate and spiraling design sat on various candle-lit desks, smoking and bubbling with an acid rainbow of mysterious chemicals. Unexplained dials and meters wagged their needles disapprovingly while an endless wyrm of copper piping hissed, angry and erratic. The whole carousel of machinery juddered and shuddered to the rhythmic clanging of a distant and nameless engine, its ringing methodical and maudlin, like a funeral knell.

It was as though a special kind of hell had been invented for all things mechanical.

"Welcome to the Factory on C12. Or, as I like to call it, Factory C12," said Riley, walking amongst the horrifying metal apparitions as though they were everyday furniture. "It may look complicated, but most of the machinery here is for fashioning tools and components.

We're a research factory first and foremost, you see—a *research* factory."

The doomsayers continued walking after the professor, unconsciously huddling together. Riley continued to chatter away in the gloom, his seesaw voice echoing from the chilly brick walls. He gestured to some of the more complex and intricate-looking machinery as he passed.

"We make all kinds of things—all *kinds* of things," he said. "We're very much left to our own devices—the advantages, I must confess, of being a royal in-law." He stopped suddenly on a platform and waited for the rest of the group to catch up. Once everybody was safely onboard, he pulled a lever, and with a furious hiss, the platform shuddered upward.

"I don't like to brag about the factory—by all that's modest, I don't like to *brag*—but we do some remarkable work here, most remarkable. I confess, I often feel like a small child in a shop that appeals to small children."

The platform came to a stop, and Riley gestured for the others to follow him through an unexceptional glass-paneled door. What lay in the next room caused his guests to stop in their tracks and gasp.

"This is my workshop," said Riley. "This is where I *create!*"

The workshop was, essentially, little more than a very large attic, lit here and there through skylights by day and overhead gas lamps by night. It was the contents of the room that made it so remarkable. On what seemed like a dozen long workbenches, devices of every conceivable shape and design lay stacked upon one another like the universe's most curious jumble sale. Cogs and gears, mirrors and pulleys, intricate-looking engines and crystals that seemed to radiate power, all lay infused within wheeled, winged, and box-like devices— devices of which Bip had never seen the like and to whose purpose he could not possibly hazard a guess. Far from the hulking, menacing machinery of the factory floor, the workshop was a crèche for myriad fantastic and unlikely-looking trinkets, each burring or buzzing in a different way, buttons and lights winking suggestively and begging— no, *demanding* the question, "What does this one do?"

"Wow," breathed Bip. There seemed little else to say.

Riley took a seat at one of the few clear spaces on the central workbench. He looked around him, as though temporarily unaware of his surroundings, then found a button in amongst the jigsaw puzzle of appliances around him. There was a *whirruk* followed by a *judud* and then a rising, raging whistle. The floor began to shake. Handen found his hand unwittingly straying to the haft of his bullwhip, and Azron assumed his characteristic pose in response to potential danger—limbs splayed so as to be ready to flee in any direction. Throughout the chaos, Riley sat with his fingers bridged and a complacent smile on his face. The whistling and shaking rose to a thunderous crescendo until finally, with a noise best described as *ka-bloink*, a squirt of oil launched from an unknown location and hit Bip squarely in the face. In the confused silence that followed, a small conveyor belt on Riley's desk began to squeak, and a plate was wheeled into view from parts unknown. It was full of little brown rectangles.

"Biscuit?" chirped Riley.

As one man, the doomsayers warily shook their heads.

THEY TALKED INTO THE NIGHT, Riley, despite the obvious fatigue of his guests, interrupting their story at every turn with questions and demands for specifics. Eventually, with darkness well and truly descended and with many a yawn stifled, their tale was told.

"Incredible," said Riley, for what seemed to be the hundredth time. "Quite, quite *incredible!*"

"So, you see what brings us to the capital?" said Handen, pinching the bridge of his nose.

"Of course, of *course!* By all that's potentially apocalyptic, of *course!*" The old man scribbled notes as he talked, a habit that was irritating at best. "Astral disaster? End of the world? Serious stuff. A most perplexing problem! One I would be most interested in working on!"

Azron raised an eyebrow. "You think you'd be able to help?"

"My good man, I was once Head of Research and Development in the department of Extremely Worrying Weaponry. If there's anyone who can destroy an errant satellite, it is I!"

"You were *once* head?" enquired Handen.

The professor seemed to momentarily lose some of his flustered enthusiasm. "I was taken off major projects after the unfortunate death of my sister. It was thought...better all 'round if I was relieved of some of my responsibilities for a time..." Riley stared hard at his notes for a moment, and when he next looked up, the former spark of enthusiasm had returned to his eye. "Still, Head of Miscellaneous and Tedious Mechanical Research has its benefits."

Handen exchanged a brief glance with Bip. Azron gave a cough that might have been a stifled laugh.

"Anyway, by all that's digressive, where was I? Ah, yes." The professor looked through some of his notes. "By my calculations coupled with your original estimation, the astral disaster, most likely, by the look of it, a meteorite roughly the size of our primary moon, will arrive in six days."

Bip, who had been verging on snoozing, suddenly sat bolt upright. "Six days?!" he said. "The world will end in six days?!"

"Approximately." Riley nodded, apparently unfazed by the revelation.

"What could we possibly do to avert a planet-wide disaster in six days?"

"Oh, I'm sure we can come up with *something*," said Riley. "After all, Argustin is the most advanced city in the world, bar none. We've the highest concentration of academic and engineering expertise on Bersch, and the resources of an intercontinental Empire at our disposal! All we'll need is the ear of the Emperor, and the culmination of many centuries of civilization will be at our aid!"

The doomsayers exchanged uncomfortable looks.

"I think we mentioned earlier..." Bip began.

"The Emperor wants us dead," finished Azron flatly.

Riley's high brow wrinkled with puzzlement. "Yes, but surely in times of great calamity, we must all work together for the common good?"

"You tell *him* that..." muttered Azron.

The professor drummed his fingers. "Far be it from me to say that the Emperor is an unreasonable man..." he began, though his eyes indicated that his mouth wasn't telling the whole truth. "I'm sure if I put in a good word, I could organize a meeting with him? Perhaps tell him of your good intentions?"

"Perhaps," agreed Handen. "But good intentions or not, we have to see him. Even if we're taken before him in chains, he has to hear what we've got to say. I need to know that your people are at least aware of the fact they stand on the verge of obliteration. After that, I've done all I can."

There was a discreet cough. "I thought we agreed that going before the Emperor in chains wasn't a good idea?" said Azron.

Handen cracked a dry smile. "That was before I knew we had six days 'til the end of everything. As it stands, in chains or otherwise, we have vital information that has ramifications for the fate of the world." He scanned the faces of his friends, slowly, as if memorizing them. "I don't expect any of you to accompany me tomorrow," he said. "Vital information or not, there is still a good chance we'll be executed after what we did to Blungkit's men. There's nothing that can't be said by one man. I won't blame anyone if they want to stay behind."

Bip shook his head. "I couldn't," he said. "There's a lot of people back home relying on me. I'd look pretty silly if I said I chickened out at the last minute."

Handen turned to Xharon, who had been mostly quiet since arriving at her father's factory. "Don't look at me," she snapped. "What kind of warrior princess would I be if I turned my back on saving the world? And besides, Uncle Tommy likes me—he might listen to you if I'm there."

Lastly, Handen turned to Azron, a questioning eyebrow raised only slightly. The thief leaned back in his chair with an unlit cigarette dangling loosely from his lower lip, absentmindedly toying with a packet of matches. "Seems to me," he began, "that if we're not all executed horribly, and the Emperor does listen to our advice, that means we're heroes." He lit the cigarette and took a long puff. "And heroes have a funny way of accumulating rewards. I'm in."

Handen grinned. "Then it's settled. Professor DeChambre will contact the Emperor's attendants tonight. With any luck, and if Riley's influence is as he claims, we should have a meeting by tomorrow morning."

Riley smiled widely. "Splendid."

Handen turned back to his comrades. "And now I suggest we all get some sleep. We'll camp here in the factory tonight, unless the professor has any objections?"

"As you wish," said Riley.

"Thank you. Now, if the rest of you want to turn in, I have something I'd like to discuss with Professor DeChambre."

Riley looked at his daughter, who merely shrugged. "Certainly," he said.

Handen waited until his friends had left the workshop, each of them cloddish with the anticipation of sleep. The door closed behind them, and the professor and the adventurer were left in the burr and purr of a multitude of mechanical watchers, standby lights blinking like a slow-motion disco against the low glow of the overhead lighting.

"These are very impressive," said Handen, pointing to one of the many heaps of devices.

"Why, thank you," said Riley, smiling. "Coming from a man who hails from another star, that's as large a compliment as I'll ever receive, I'll warrant."

Handen nodded and continued to scan the various trinkets. One in particular caught his attention, the angular shapes leaping out instantly to his soldier's perception. He picked out two pistolas, larger and more unwieldy than the one he wore at his belt. Frowning with inquisitive satisfaction, he weighed the weapons in his hands, checking the sights in turn.

"That's one of the trinkets I was working on when I was Head of Weapons," said Riley. "Both are capable of firing rapid successive shots with little loss of accuracy or power. They're prototypes, by all that's experimental—*prototypes*. I never had the chance to showcase them to the Board of Admissions. A shame, really, an innovative design. You see the real ingenuity is not in the actual weapon design but in—"

"The ammunition," finished Handen. "The ballast is encased with the charge and ignition, meaning no flint, flash-pan, or separate powder."

Riley faltered. "Yes. Erm...you've seen one before, have you?"

Handen didn't take his eyes off the pistola. "I've seen weapons the likes of which you couldn't conceive, Professor. Not in your most dangerous of nightmares. Spiritguns, Clawshanks, Razorhawks. Weapons that leave no trace of living tissue, or weapons that evaporate only armor." Handen lowered the pistolas back to the table, where they sat with the weighty promise that is the hallmark of all firearms across the ultraverse. "Tell me, Professor, what does this device do?" He pointed to a looped and soapy-looking machine situated next to the guns. It belched wetly at random intervals.

"That? Oh, that's a trinket I was working on just the other day." Riley leaned over and flicked a switch. The machine began to vibrate, then suddenly, with a mechanical hiccup, blew a bubble into the air. Several others followed until a long stream of soapy spheres spluttered gently into the workshop, bursting with quiet enthusiasm as they hit the floor. "It's for children. You know—parties and things," said Riley, grinning.

Handen smiled a humorless smile as the bumbling professor tried to turn off the suddenly overenthusiastic party machine. He was beginning to form a picture of the intellect before him.

Handen doubted that throughout the professor's career as Head of Extremely Worrying Weaponry, he had once considered the lives lost to his creations. Such men were dangerous. Such men could be the end of worlds...or, perhaps, their saviors.

The adventurer dismissed the thought, focusing his tired mind on the situation at hand.

"Tell me," he began. "What is the Emperor like?"

Riley turned from the bubble machine, an expression of shocked surprise flashing over his face. "The Emperor...is a glorious ruler. Well-loved by the people."

"Yeah, I figured that would be the official standing, but you must know him more personally than that. He was married to your sister, wasn't he?"

"Yes...yes, of course."

"So?"

"Well...he was awfully fond of weapons. Always had lots of ideas. Some of them quite outside the realms of probability but some of them...just realistic enough to be...very productive."

Handen sighed. "Look, Riley, you know why I'm here. I'm not a spy or an informant. If everything goes as planned, I have a meeting tomorrow with the most powerful man on the planet, who, for some reason, wants me dead. You've worked for this man! You're his *in-law*, for gods' sake! Now, call me pedantic if you like, but I think it might be proper to have some information about him before we meet."

Riley looked at the floor again. When he looked up, there was a pained focus in his expression that hadn't been there before.

"He's mad," said the professor. "By all that's terrifying, he's as mad as the eye of hell."

Handen nodded as if he had expected the answer. He motioned for the professor to continue.

"He's dangerous—a very dangerous man. He has no regard for human life! Some of the things he did when I worked with him...I was always safe because I was useful—that was why he made me a duke— but others... Others... He would kill and have them killed without blinking, with no anger, no sorrow—just a kind of...impatience..."

"You think he'll listen to us?" asked Handen.

Riley removed his multi-lensed glasses and began nervously polishing them with a handkerchief. "I couldn't say. He may be insane, but he isn't stupid. He has the finest minds on Bersch in his employ. If *we* know that there is a meteorite approaching, it's more than likely *he* knows. But no matter what information you claim to have, even if you thought you *could* save the planet, there's no guaranteeing that the Emperor will hear you. If he wants you dead—*truly* wants you dead—

then he may listen to your case, smile, nod, click his fingers, and then...you'll never be seen again."

Handen stared hard at the man. "It's a risk I'll have to take," he said after a while.

The professor nodded. He seemed to have calmed down, though his face was sheened with sweat. "You've no idea how good it felt to say all those things. If the Emperor were to hear one word of treachery, they would come for me in the night. I would disappear, and no one would even bother to ask about me because too many questions would make them disappear as well. By all that's paranoid, I've not dared to speak my mind about the Emperor in all my life, even when Yvette died..." The professor looked up from his polishing and directly at Handen. A slow tear gathered at the corner of his wrinkled eye. "They said it was a weak heart, but Yvette was as strong as an ox, by all that's vital—*as strong as an ox!*"

"You think she was killed?"

Riley shook his head slowly. "I didn't at first. You see, my wife, Tilla, died when Xharon was just a little girl. Yvette helped to raise her after that...helped me when I thought I couldn't go on. When she married the Emperor, we were all happy for her, none so more than I." The professor paused, peering into black memory. "When she died, I found it hard to let her go. I started asking questions, interviewing the castle physicians over and over, desperate to find out how someone as strong and vital and as beautiful as Yvette could have just...died. With no former complaints, just...died. I asked too many questions. I was demoted, and it was made very clear to me that my questions would have to stop."

"I see," said Handen.

"I brushed up on my history—the history of the Draegul succession. Queens very rarely get a mention in Argustin law, but they all have one trait in common—they all die young, only a couple of years after their marriage."

"You think homicide runs in the family?"

The professor shrugged. "I think the Emperor is a truly evil man from a long line of truly evil men. I think that if he wanted *me* dead, I'd be as far from the Empire as possible."

The two men held each other's gaze. "You understand I have to go through with this meeting?" said Handen.

"Of course. I shall visit with the night clerk at Dawncastle. If there is to be a meeting, you will know by tomorrow afternoon."

Handen paused for a moment. "Would you like me to leave Xharon behind?"

Riley chuckled and shook his head. "I doubt you'd be able to if you wanted to. Besides, 'Uncle Tommy' *is* rather...amused by her. She might be able to help your case."

"And you?"

The professor shook his head again. "I will relay my findings to the proper authorities. I no longer hold a position in which I may report directly to the Emperor."

"Understood," said Handen. "And now, if you'll excuse me, I think I'll turn in for the night."

"Of course, of course," said Riley, appearing his usual flustered self, the melancholy seemingly forgotten in his absentmindedness. "You'd better get some rest—by all that's exhausted, you'll need your *rest*."

Handen waved and left, shutting the door behind him. Riley sat back at his workbench, taking refuge in the soft tweetings of his creations. He sighed deeply. "By all that's holy, you'll need all the rest you can get."

BIP STARED up at the storeroom ceiling. It was warm and comfortable near the boiler, and the distant clanging of the factory quarter was oddly lulling, but despite it all, sleep still eluded the Kaneqian. He watched Xharon, pencil-sketched in the orange glow of the firelight as she went about the nightly ritual of polishing her axes. In accordance with her father's constant pleas, Xharon had reluctantly donned a nightie—a high-collared, flowery affair that covered every inch of skin bar her face and hands. The transformation was quite astonishing. Xharon seemed instantly younger, more fragile and feminine and, thought a steadfast part of Bip's libido, less interesting to look at.

As much as it was strange to see her preparing warrior weapons in this chokingly modest attire, it was stranger still to be sharing a roof with her. Even though the princess lay a good ten feet away, something about the intimacy of sleeping within the same four walls was causing Bip to lie wide awake when, by rights, he should be resting.

Something stirred in the young Kaneqian as he watched his companion go about her nightly routine. Whether born of the soft light of the strange surroundings or perhaps of the anxiety felt for the coming day, there was something dreamlike and subdued about the whole scene. Something he might have called magical, had he been more familiar with the term.

"Xharon?" he said, and was amazed by how harsh his voice seemed in the relative silence.

Xharon paused and looked up. "Yes?"

"Are you worried about tomorrow?"

"No. Why would I be?"

Bip frowned. "In case we all get executed..."

"Oh, that," said Xharon. "I don't think that will happen."

"Really? How can you be so sure?"

"Well, I don't know—things have worked out for the best so far, haven't they?"

Oh, yes, thought Bip, *everything works out fine until it doesn't, and that's when the worrying starts...*

"Why do you ask?" said Xharon.

Bip blinked. "No reason, really. It's just, you know, if you were worried, it'd be okay..."

"But I'm not."

"Yes, but if you were, you know, I'd understand."

"I'm not worried."

Bip raised his hands. "All right, okay, I just thought I'd say that it's okay to be worried if you want to. There's no shame in it."

The two doomsayers sat in the flickering glow of the boiler, listening to the sound of Azron's quiet snoring and the distant noise of machinery clanking with melancholy persistence.

"Are *you* worried?" said Xharon unexpectedly.

Bip flustered, caught unaware. "Me? Worried? No. No, of course not."

"Even though there's a good chance you'll be put to death tomorrow?"

"No. No, I'm fine, really."

"Even though it could be a very, very *slow* death?"

Bip began to sweat. Perhaps the boiler was a bit too hot. "I'm okay with it, thanks," he said.

In the low light of the room, Bip thought he saw the corners of Xharon's lips rise in a small, secret smile.

"You're quite brave, you know," she said.

Bip tried to ignore the sudden fluttery feeling in his chest. "Really? Why do you say that?"

The princess began counting on her fingers. "Well, for a start, you're not very big, are you? And you obviously can't fight, and you don't really have any sort of special skills, do you? And when all's said and done, you're a bit of a wimp..."

"Sorry, is this supposed to be making me feel better?" interrupted Bip.

Xharon laughed. "And despite all those things, you've traveled halfway across the world, taken on everything in your path, escaped certain death on several occasions, and tomorrow...tomorrow you go to confront the most powerful man in the civilized world, who, incidentally, has spent the last few months crafting your doom. When you think about it like that, you're pretty gosh-darn brave."

Bip grinned, his face flushing. "Yes. Yes, I suppose I am."

He ducked as a shoe suddenly sailed past his head.

"You'll be pretty gosh-darn beaten up if you don't stop talking and let me get some sleep," growled Azron. "Honestly, go and take a cold shower, why don't you?"

Xharon blushed a pretty pink and pulled the blanket over her head. Bip sat up for a while, grinning at nothing in particular until, lulled by the sleep-sounds of his friends, he nodded off.

HANDEN SAT AWAKE, darning a hole in his last good shirt. Riley had offered to lend him some clothes, but Handen doubted any garment belonging to the portly professor would fit him well.

He knew he wouldn't sleep tonight; he had caught a few catnaps here and there but was too restless to doze for more than a couple of minutes at a time. Every cell in his body was preparing for tomorrow's confrontation—a confrontation that could not be fought with blades and bullets, only with words and reason. And after that, who knew?

He brought out the waterskin containing the dregs of the fountain of death. Even now, the leather decanter was looking aged and deteriorated. Handen doubted it would last much longer under its deeply unnatural burden. Tomorrow, then, or perhaps the day after. Leave enough time to help if he could, and then...and then he would drink.

Handen sighed and placed the waterskin at his side. Then he began the process of disarming himself. It took some time.

THE NEW DAY came as any other, with no significant fanfare, no special formality, and devoid of omens of any kind. The sun rose, and the world spun on regardless. The day came as any other—apart from the new star, which hung low and steadfast and fat with ill promise.

Bip was awoken by the morning shift whistle, and by the stomp of a thousand workers' boots, and by the various mechanical yawns of an army of machines preparing for a new day of labor. He had looked out of the storeroom window onto the streets of the factory quarter, impressed as countless regiments of boiler-suited workmen flooded the streets, smoking, chatting, and filtering off into their various places of work. If they were at all concerned about the new, pale light in the morning sky, they didn't show it.

Awaiting news from Riley, the doomsayers had taken the morning to prepare for their visit to court, taking it in turns to scrub off months of ingrained road dirt in an old tin bath, and washing and repairing their clothes. Xharon, who had reluctantly revealed her skills in needlework, had offered to darn any holes, while Bip and Azron had taken turns scrubbing clothes with an old washboard and several dozen tubs of hot water.

Bip had done his best with the clothes he had left Kaneq in. Though his heavy jumper was now too full of holes to wear respectfully, his gray undershirt and canvas slacks needed only an hour or so with a needle and a few bars of soap. Azron had managed to scrub his long coat back from the dust-colored gray it had become to the midnight blue it had once been, and Handen looked like a very formal pirate in a billowy white shirt and brown leather trousers. Certainly, he looked less threatening without his heavy coat and innumerable scabbards, buckles, and holsters. The only item he had insisted on keeping about his person was the rotting waterskin containing the waters of the fountain of death, something he felt he could not leave behind.

The three stood—shaved and scrubbed, looking as clean as they had before taking to the road—and nervously waited for their summons. Bip felt unusual. Without Brian by his side and his heavy, worn rucksack on his back, he felt lighter and oddly naked. He could only imagine how the disarmed Handen felt.

At that moment, the storeroom door swung open and, as one man, they turned...and gaped. If Xharon had understood the term "formal attire," she had understood it in an extremely unique way.

"...!" said Bip.

"...!" agreed Azron.

"What the hell is that supposed to be?" cried Handen.

Xharon twirled. "Don't you like it?"

The outfit had ghostly echoes of the formal attire expected of the ladies of the Argustin court. There were certainly frills and lace and other things you might expect...though the frills erupted from the bottom of a polished metal brassiere with inappropriately placed spikes, and the lace was merely a thin gauze barely covering what appeared to be a pair of bearskin underpants. The full effect of the outfit was amplified somewhat by the thigh-high leather riding boots, the enormous metal shoulder pads, and the highly-polished helm from the sides of which metal wings arced aerodynamically.

"It's...it's very you," said Bip weakly.

"Isn't it, though?" said Xharon. "Of course, the Turnmisin swamp she-warriors don't really have a precedent for formal occasions, so I had to improvise."

"You certainly did that..." muttered Azron.

"And what is *that?*" asked Handen.

"What?" replied Xharon, eyes wide and innocent.

"In your hand."

Xharon looked down at the four-foot long battle-axe she was leaning on. "Oh, this? This is just an accessory," she said.

"No weapons," said Handen firmly. "We agreed."

"I can't make a public appearance without at least one weapon! I'll be a laughing stock!"

Azron coughed and looked at the floor.

"What did you say?" said Xharon, her eyes narrowing.

"Oh, nothing, nothing. Nothing at all," replied Azron, looking about to avoid meeting Xharon's gaze.

"No weapons," Handen reiterated. "You can leave it here."

Xharon huffed and let the axe fall to the floor with a clang.

"Look!" cried Bip. The doomsayers turned to the Kaneqian, who was peering out of the wide storeroom window. "They're here."

Down below, on the streets of the factory quarter, Professor Riley DeChambre approached, flanked by two Regulators and followed by a line of black-and-silver armored soldiers, wielding the largest flint-locks Bip had ever seen.

"It's time to meet the Emperor, then," he said faintly.

The others watched in silence at the approach of the Imperial Guard.

HANDEN LED THE WAY, slamming open the doors of Factory C12 as dramatically as he could.

"Well?" he demanded.

Riley gestured apologetically at the armed men behind him. On closer inspection, the Regulators seemed taller and broader than those the doomsayers had encountered so far, though the familiar expression of malice still characterized their features. As butch as the Regulators appeared, however, they were nearly dwarfed by the bulk of the black-clad guards behind them, their bulbous armor and full-face helms making them look like extremely well-armed beetles.

"The Emperor has granted you an audience," said Riley.

Handen eyed the soldiers mistrustfully. "Are we to be taken before him in chains?"

"Oh no, no. By all that's misunderstood, these are merely your *escort.*"

The immortal allowed a doubtful smirk to saunter across his face. "Very well," he said. "Lead the way."

"If you would be so good as to follow me, Mr. Strike?" said Riley, bowing politely.

The companions fell in step with Riley, trying to ignore the guards as they fell into position, surrounding them. They began walking at an even stroll, Bip trying not to appear intimidated by the colossal guardsmen who paced him.

Riley leaned closer to Handen. "I'm so sorry, but he insisted on sending them, though he did clarify that they were merely for your protection," he whispered.

Handen smirked again. "Protection from whom?"

"It is rumored that there are dangerous people roaming the streets —some sort of unusual cult who are, or so I've heard, obsessed with the end of the world."

Handen paused suddenly, ignoring the sound of a dozen weapons being gripped more firmly by the Imperial guards behind him. "So, then...the people know?"

Riley shrugged. "I am unsure exactly *what* they know."

"It seems they know enough. Perhaps the Emperor will have no choice but to hear us now."

"We can but hope," agreed the professor.

The party set off, walking to the rhythm of the clanking armor of their escort.

LEAVING the factory quarter and entering the city proper, they might as well have been entering another world. Gone were the regimented streets and the flat, soulless buildings. Gone were the smog and cobbles, replaced instead by smooth, marble-like roads, mosaic-patterned pavements, and tall, seamless glass buildings that you had to crane your neck to see the top of. The people changed, too, of course. The fabulously dressed and impossibly beautiful citizens of Argustin laughed in the streets or sipped coffee in umbrella-studded bistros. They lined up outside grandiose theatres or went about their business in sharp, elegant suits, glancing casually at expensive pocket watches. They were a far cry from the grim and busy factory workers. They were, in fact, almost the complete opposite.

Bip and Azron had both marveled at the level of technology in the city, steam devices and engine carts appearing with a frequency that totally outclassed what they had seen in Panthalus. Propeller-driven monorails rode on stick-thin railings far above their heads, and city rail trains wove gracefully along their polished guide-tracks. The ballet of city traffic flowed without a hitch, carefully monitored by narrow-eyed Regulators on horseback while intricate, colored gas-lamps ordered HALT and PROCEED at seemingly random intervals.

The Kaneqian watched as a gaggle of students, resplendent in their black academic gowns, rolled laughingly into a wine bar, guffawing and hee-hawing over some comical irony. On the other side of the street, impeccable businessmen in silk ties and long-tails stepped onto a steam-powered glass elevator that hissed with great speed to the top floor of an important-looking building.

In this skyline of spires, arches and towers, the crystalline mountain of Dawncastle shone like another sun, bathing Argustin in a pale, lovely pink and drawing the eye ever upward.

"Nice place," said Bip, flatly.

"Nah," said Azron. "It's got no soul to it! Where's the street life? Where's the character? Where's the robbery?"

"Robbery?" gasped Xharon. "Oh, we don't tolerate that sort of thing in the city. If you can't afford to live here properly, you're deported. It's a very effective system."

"Yeah, I'll bet," said Azron, bitterly.

The city gates had been extremely heavily guarded, every potential entrant checked thoroughly by intimidating men with axes. Handen had commented that, without Xharon's help, they would never have been able to enter the city. Azron, who made a living by getting into places he wasn't allowed, had disagreed.

The troupe made its way through the streets of Argustin as both traffic and pedestrians wisely gave way to the armed contingent. Bip couldn't resist looking upward at the enormous and polished buildings that surrounded him. It was a hallmark of civilization unique in his experience, and he wondered who would possibly want to live so high up.

Eventually, he looked back down to street level, if only to ease the ache in his neck. It was then that he saw the commotion on the streets —a thin gray line of Regulators stood arm-in-arm against a small but surging crowd. The people in the crowd didn't look as if they belonged in Argustin at all; they had a general grubbiness about them that suggested they were well-traveled and little-washed. They were wearing identical red robes and shouting and struggling and generally seemed pretty upset about something. Bip strained his ears to hear what was going on.

"Voice of the Prophet...! Terrible Custard...! End of the world is nigh...! You're standing on my foot! Verily...arrrgh!"

A sudden memory jolted in Bip's head. He began scanning the faces of the struggling crowd, peering through his glasses until he found the face he had been half expecting. At the front of the crowd and doing what she did best was Celia Doom, the speaker from Panthalus. She was screaming with the same shrill zeal she had when Bip had heard her months ago, her dirty face and blond hair a rallying point for the rest of the red-robed mob.

"Warning from the ancient ones…We will be heard! Behold…! The hooded adolescent of fear is standing outside the corner shop of inevitability! Get your finger out of my eye, you bastard!"

"My word!" exclaimed Bip.

Handen looked back. "What is it?"

"That girl!" Bip pointed to the struggling throng. "She's Celia Doom! The one I told you about? The one I talked to just before I got arrested!"

Handen smiled. "Unbelievable. She's come all this way." He turned to Riley. "Are these the dangerous people you were told about?"

The professor nodded. "Apparently they've sprung up all over the continent. They call themselves the Cult of the Doomsayer, by all that's ominous."

Handen chuckled and turned back to Bip, clapping him on the shoulder. "Well done, kid. You've spread the word. In fact, you've completed the mission I set out to complete centuries ago—you've warned civilization that the end of the world is coming."

"Still," said Bip, looking up at the pale light in the sky, which even now seemed to grow bigger. "I may have left it a bit late."

Handen shrugged. "If we do all we can, what more can we do? Now, let's go and see this Emperor. If he hasn't got the message by now, he's even more of a psychopath than I've heard."

Beside the former Hostilities Advisor, an Imperial guard cocked the hammer on his flintlock rifle. There was a tense silence, which was thankfully broken by a shrill yelp. Celia had noticed them.

"It's him!" she screamed. "It is the prophet of the Ancient Ones! He who has been delivered unto us to deliver a message…unto us! Get off me! Get off!"

The ragged girl struggled as two Regulators lifted her into the air. She reached out to Bip as she was carried away.

"Help us, Doomsayer! Tell them the end of days is upon us!"

Bip shrugged. "I don't think they'll listen," he said, and gestured to the armed guards who surrounded him.

"Oh…" said Celia as she was carried into the distance. "Bugger."

They watched as the girl was carried away, and the rest of the Cult of the Doomsayer either fled or were rounded up by the remaining Regulators.

"I think we'd better get moving, yes? Wouldn't like to keep the Emperor waiting, by all that's punctual—we wouldn't want to keep him *waiting*," said Riley.

The Imperial guard who had readied his weapon lowered it again and motioned for Handen to walk. The adventurer did and, followed closely by his companions, set off for the gates of Dawncastle.

3

Interlude: Everyday Heroes.

Backtracking the crisscross trail of Bip and Handen, far and away from Argustin, Kaneq sat as it always had, forever huddled against the brutality of the Ice Plains. Here, the farthest point from the solar system's resident star, the new silver light in the sky—that harbinger of certain sorrow—was obscured by the bulk of Bersch. Thus, even the most wise and ancient of the Kaneqians sat unaware that their apocalyptic deadline had been unexpectedly brought forward. Not that it could have made much difference—the citizens and the final chosen had done nothing but work flat-out since they had heard the dread news, and no cosmic threat, no matter how terrifying, could have motivated them more.

Though perhaps if Bailey had known, he wouldn't have been sitting as relaxed as he was now, his feet propped on a table, a pipe hanging lazily from his mouth. He sat in the Empty Goat, which was living up to its name (due to the fact that it was empty, not that it was a goat).

Behind the bar, Michaelmas was polishing glasses and whistling a distracted and broken tune. Bailey took a long pull from the steel tankard before him and smacked his lips with satisfaction.

He had changed considerably in a short time, the strenuous and brutal training regime filling out his soft bulk with unprecedented muscle, straightening his hunched frame, and bringing color into his normally sickly skin. His long hair was tied back in a tight ponytail, and his stubbled jaw had grown into a thin, cropped beard. But despite the noticeable improvements in his health and appearance, he wouldn't have traded tomorrow morning's break for anything. Tonight might be his last opportunity to drink, and drink he would.

He drained the tankard and signaled for a refill, lighting his pipe as he awaited fresh ale.

He had come through the physical training, unexpectedly, with flying colors. Once he'd got over his sporadic coughing fits, he had shown a prowess with weaponry and a level of fitness that had impressed even Rynford, and he had muddled well enough through his psyentific training to receive the bare minimum of praise from Glimton. Consequently, he and a few others had been given a morning off for some leisure time before the day the volunteers would leave—or V-Day, as it had come to be known.

The overall volunteer party consisted of about fifty individuals of varying ages and backgrounds, though mostly youngsters. There were some who exceled in psyence, some who had been selected from the hunting party, and some who had been chosen purely on the basis of their ingenuity and resourcefulness. Others had proven themselves useful, some with quite unexpected skills. Half-Brick, for instance, had shown an uncanny knack for sailing—unusual for a boy who had never before seen a boat. It was even rumored that a few elders had made the chosen.

Now that the final group had been selected, craftsmen and psyentists were putting the finishing touches to the four boats that would carry them across the Cold Ocean. The next few days would be spent preparing the volunteers for an ocean journey with some trial runs in the boats, while those who still showed weakness in certain areas were to be given last-minute tutelage and training.

For now, though, a few of the volunteers had been granted a brief reprieve to spend with their friends, family, or in Bailey's case, with the pub.

He sucked thoughtfully on his pipe and looked down at the heavy bow and arrow that he carried everywhere with him these days. It was a hulking and many-stringed affair, designed for felling thick-muscled snow beasts from safe distances. It was a weapon not often used by the hunters of Kaneq, but one Bailey had shown particular prowess with, so he had been given it as his own. He smiled to think that, only a few weeks ago, he had barely been able to pull back and draw. Now, thanks to near-constant practice and Rynford's training, he was an accomplished marksman.

He wondered how many of the other volunteers were sitting surprised at themselves—those who had been nothing more than lumberjacks or tanners, suddenly heroes on whom the fate of the world depended. He wondered if this was how Bip must have felt. He wondered more how scared his friend must have been to have had suffered this responsibility on his own with no one to confide in and with no support from the community. He wondered if Bip had felt as scared as *he* felt now. Bailey sucked thoughtfully on his pipe, and then dismissed the notion. There would be plenty of time for anxiety later. Now, it was time to drink.

He smiled as Michaelmas wordlessly placed another tankard on the table, then he raised his drink in a brief salute before downing half the ale in one. Tomorrow he would be a hero. Today he was going to get as drunk as humanly possible.

He paused mid-quaff as the door to the Empty Goat flew open, letting in a chill breeze. Most of the psyentists were occupied with the preparations for V-Day, which meant that the heatshield was not being maintained at its usual strength. Thus, Kaneq was experiencing an early winter, and a few flakes of snow drifted onto the pub floor, where they melted with quiet relief. Wheeling himself slowly with a familiar squeak of heavy axels, Truggle rowed his way into the pub.

Michaelmas blinked. It was not often that Kaneq's most senior was seen out and about by himself.

"Can I help ye, sire?" he said.

Truggle rowed to the bar. "Something strong and large," he said.

Michaelmas complied, pouring a double measure of brandy from one of the more expensive bottles. He passed it carefully to Truggle, who downed the sweet spirit in one.

"Another," he said.

Bailey watched with interest. Since informing the community of the impending astral disaster, Truggle had dropped his befuddled old man act and had revealed a lucid and sharp mind, a fact that had shocked and surprised many of Kaneq's residents, Bailey included.

He watched as the old man drank his drink, slowly this time, sipping rather than gulping. Warmed by alcohol, the normally morose Bailey felt moved to conversation.

"Drinking alone, sir?"

The elder turned to the younger man. "The best way sometimes. You too, I see."

Bailey nodded. "A lot to think about, I suppose."

Truggle cracked a humorless grin. "Certainly. The end of the world tends to occupy one's thoughts quite selfishly."

Bailey returned the grin. "Yes, I suppose so. Still, at least we're doing something about it. It's not long 'til V-Day. There's still hope."

"Hope?" Truggle chuckled mirthlessly. "Sending our children into the wilderness is hope?"

Bailey frowned, clearly annoyed. "There's fifty of us. All highly trained, all prepared for the worst. Surely there's a good chance we can reach the mainland?"

"There have been many brave men and women who have ventured into the wilds over the centuries—stronger hunters than Rynford, more cunning psyentists than Glimton and certainly far wiser men than I. None of these heroes ever returned, yet you're certain that a group of youths with a few months' training will succeed where Kaneq's elite have failed countless times?"

There was a long silence.

"If what you say is true," began Bailey, speaking through clenched teeth. "If it really is so hopeless, then why send Bip? Why send one boy out to certain death?"

For a while, Truggle didn't reply. "I had faith in the boy," he said eventually. "I still do." With that, he placed his glass carefully on the bar and rowed his way toward the exit. "Goodnight to you all, and good luck to you, young Bailey. I mean that." The old man rowed out into the dark night.

Bailey shivered, putting it down to the sudden chill. He paused for a while, staring at nothing. Then he reached for his tankard.

"Not very positive, is he?" said the volunteer.

Michaelmas nodded. "He was about Bip. Seemed convinced the lad was going to go far."

Bailey considered his ale for a moment. "No offense, Michaelmas—Bip was my friend, and a good friend he was too—but we can't rely on his success. It's madness to sit back and pin our hopes on one boy, let alone Bip."

Michaelmas nodded again. "I suppose so."

Bailey stared into his pint again, a tear coming unbidden to his eye. "Do you think he's alive?"

Michaelmas said nothing.

Bailey rose slowly to his feet and made to leave.

"Not finishing your drink?" said Michaelmas.

Bailey shook his head. "I've lost the taste for it."

LATER, in the bowels of the Dome, alone in the dim and eerie light, Truggle sat watching a set of flickering numbers as they counted down.

"I still have faith," he whispered.

4

A Grudge Match Centuries in the Making...

The doomsayers walked through the Imperial gardens, silent with their own thoughts as the shining pinnacle of Dawncastle loomed ever closer. Bip could not help but marvel at the beauty that surrounded him. It put even Ted's garden to shame.

The gardens of Dawncastle were exactly as one would expect—huge, ornate, delicate, and neat. Fountains and rose beds studded wide expanses of perfectly flat lawn. Here and there, gravel pathways converged with beautifully crafted bridges sailing over mirror-like ponds, the surfaces of which were disturbed only by the occasional bite of a rare and expensive fish. Domesticated wildlife roamed the grounds, eyeing newcomers with docile curiosity and lolloping between islands of carefully woven plants and flowers, each rare and colorful petal arranged with painstaking delicacy and exquisite taste. Statues popped up here and there like frozen wanderers, each marble rendition a perfect idolization of woman, man, or beast.

It was easy to be awed by the Imperial gardens, to feel that perhaps here man and nature had combined in the most perfect way imaginable to create a small slice of paradise. It took the cynical minds of the solider and the thief to see the dark genius behind it all...

For starters, the garden lay between an outer wall and Dawncastle's inner wall, surrounding the palace completely and meaning that anyone wishing to approach would have to traverse a wide area without much cover, leaving them vulnerable to searchlights and the marksmen manning the inner wall. Gravel was difficult to cross noiselessly, and Handen had recognized some of the rare and expensive fish in the pond as piranha. He had no doubt that some of the meandering wildlife was trained to attack on sight. He also realized that the pathways and ponds and rivers crisscrossed in a way that meant an intruder couldn't walk toward the palace in a straight line from any direction. There were obstacles to be crossed from all angles. Finally, Azron was pretty sure that at least some of the statues they had passed, usually the ones with weapons, were breathing…

These observations, coupled with the myriad unseen booby-traps that more than likely peppered the pathways they weren't currently taking, meant the gardens, while beautiful to look at, were a very effective trap for potential assassins or thieves.

Handen entertained dark thoughts. Insane tyrant or not, the Emperor was no fool.

After walking for a good twenty minutes, they finally arrived at the main entrance of Dawncastle, a huge wooden door encased in the surrounding glasswork like a fly in amber. As they approached, one of the escorting Regulators advanced and knocked his truncheon on the door with three loud bangs. After a while, a window opened in the woodwork, out of which popped a small face with a bulbous nose, wearing an expression of extreme harassment. The man wore a green furry hat that verged on the ridiculous and hid his mouth behind a moustache that bristled with self-importance.

"What's this? Who goes there?" said the gatekeeper, in a voice that seemed to suggest he was an important man with important bits of paper to look at, and that this interruption was an encroachment on something that was, undoubtedly, very important.

"It is I," boomed the Regulator, "Patrol Constable Jargette."

"And who are these people with you?" demanded the gatekeeper, his voice almost comically suspicious.

"They have come to see the Emperor."

The gatekeeper's eyes widened dramatically. "What?! See the Emperor? No one sees the Emperor! Not no one, not no how!"

There was a brief silence before Jargette coughed. He leaned up, speaking so quietly to the gatekeeper that Bip had to concentrate hard to hear what was being said.

"Actually, Dave, they really *are* here to see the Emperor."

The gatekeeper, or Dave as he had been revealed, frowned in puzzlement. "Not no one, not no how?" he ventured.

The Regulator coughed again, apparently embarrassed. "I'm serious, Dave. You can drop the tourist thing. These people *really do* have an appointment with the Emperor."

"Oh," said Dave. "Oh. Really. Well, why didn't you say so?"

The gatekeeper disappeared, the hatch slamming shut behind him. Jargette coughed and regained his composure. He rapped smartly three times on the massive doors, and this time, with a loud, metallic groan, they opened, as slow and certain as a distant tidal wave.

Bip squinted as he was bathed in a warm light. It seemed unnatural that the inside of a room should be brighter and warmer than the midday sun outside, but this was exactly the case as the warped, twisted, and redirected sunlight beamed through every glass panel of Dawncastle's intricate and uncanny architecture until, magnified and amplified, it gushed languidly from the front door.

"The Emperor awaits you in the reception hall," Jargette said bluntly, and led the way inside.

The doomsayers entered, stepping into a giant hallway that seemed to be constructed of warm, pink ice. Bip gaped in awe as his eye was drawn upward to a glass ceiling tinted a fiery yellow, and beyond that a further glass ceiling, this one slightly orange. The ceilings continued past Bip's low perspective, presumably, right to the top of Dawncastle. He felt uncomfortably dizzy as he saw the faint silhouettes of people walking around several hundred meters above him.

His attention was drawn back to ground level by a discreet cough. Seemingly from nowhere, Dave the gatekeeper had reappeared, this time on top of a cart pulled by a donkey. For some reason, the donkey had been dyed various different colors. Whether or not the donkey was pleased about this was difficult to say. Donkeys rarely seem pleased by anything.

"Erm…I don't suppose you wanted to ride on the Donkey of Many Colors, did you?" said Dave.

Jargette sighed heavily. "God dammit, Dave, I told you—they're not tourists!"

"I have a song and everything!"

"Just sod off, will you?"

Dejected, Dave led the rainbow-painted donkey back the way he had come, humming a sad little song as he left. The doomsayers and escorts alike stood around in embarrassed silence.

"Erm… This way to the reception hall," mumbled Jargette, once again taking the lead.

"Why can't we ride the donkey?" whispered Xharon. "*I want to ride the donkey!*"

They followed Jargette through the massive hallway and a series of crystal corridors until they arrived at another huge set of doors. Unlike the main entrance, these doors were protected by a dozen of the thickly armored Imperial guardsmen, who simultaneously saluted and sidestepped as the group approached, adjusting their postures to something that merely hinted at the possibility of violence, rather than guaranteeing it. The doors opened almost silently, as though hushed by the sheer enormity of the occasion.

"I'm afraid this is where I must leave you all," said Riley, his voice sudden and apologetic. "The Emperor has only granted audience for the four of you. My presence is not desired, by all that's uninvited—not *desired*."

Handen clapped him on the shoulder. "Don't worry about it. We know what we have to do."

Bip coughed and leaned close to the professor. "If we…you know… if things don't go as planned, someone needs to try…something. Anything."

Riley nodded. "I'll do everything in my power to find a solution, but the Emperor really is our best hope." The older man shook each of the doomsayer's hands solemnly in turn until, reaching Xharon, he embraced her in an awkward hug. "Try not to get yourself into any trouble, dear," he said.

Xharon rolled her eyes. "Oh, *Daddy.*"

"And couldn't you have at least found a nice dress to wear?"

"Daddy, *please!* Not in front of the minions!"

Riley shook his head and began heading back down the corridor they had come from. "Good luck to you all," he called, his voice echoing lifelessly against the glass-brick walls.

The doomsayers stood for a while, watching as Riley DeChambre waddled from view, then they turned to one another.

"Well," said Bip. "I suppose this is it."

"It's not too late to leg it," said Azron. "Say the word and I could be out of those doors before these mugs could say, 'Stop that really fast thief!'"

"I wish you'd let me bring my battle-axe," said Xharon.

Handen nodded agreement. Every cell in his millennium-year-old body was telling him that they were walking into danger, and his fingers kept gripping at handles and shafts that were no longer there.

"Bip?" he said. "Do you want to lead?"

Bip blinked in surprise. "Me? I sort of envisioned *you* leading the way, really."

Handen shook his head. "I'm no diplomat," he said. "I think you might be more suited to this."

Bip looked, in turn, at each of his new friends and spoke hesitantly. "If you think I can do it."

"Of course you can," said Xharon.

"Rather you than me, guv," said Azron.

Bip took a deep breath. "Then let's go."

AS SOON AS he entered the reception hall, Handen felt faint. He wondered at first if this was genuine fear, an emotion he had learned to suppress and ignore centuries ago, but as he followed his comrades down the length of an elaborately woven red carpet, he realized that he had been feeling a similar sensation quite frequently since his release from the Bin…though never as potent as this.

As they traversed the floor of the gigantic hall, the disturbing feeling amplified, triggered by the sight of comparatively mundane things—a figure on a particular portrait, the color and pattern of the wallpaper, or the faint tinkling sound of the chandelier that hung high overhead. Of all these things, however, nothing made the sensation peak more dramatically than the sight of the thin, black-and-silver-clad figure sitting on the massive gold-wrought throne at the head of the room. It was the Emperor Draegul.

Suddenly Handen could put a name to the stomach-clenching feeling he was experiencing. It was *déjà vu*, the feeling that he had been here once before. Having roamed much of the world in days too long ago to remember, the immortal was used to the feeling, but never had he experienced it as strongly as he did now. He felt as though he were tiptoeing near the edges of a half-remembered epoch, as though a terrible enlightenment flickered just a shadow's breath away. Something was scratching at the doors of his subconscious, demanding recognition, something dark and terrible that would not desist. He shivered, the world around him suddenly seeming paper-thin, spinning on an axis far away from his own.

He jumped as he felt a hand on his arm and looked down into Xharon's concerned eyes.

"Are you all right?" she asked.

Handen nodded, making an effort to regain his composure. It was difficult. He felt as if he were going to pass out at any minute. As if he were constantly falling.

Ahead of Handen, Bip led the way. He was doing his best to maintain a steady and confident march toward the Emperor but, as was usually the case when one concentrated too hard on what was generally an automatic function, he had forgotten how to walk. The Emperor's expression wasn't helping matters. He was smiling like a cat watching a mouse commit suicide.

Bip turned back toward his friends, seeking confidence there. They weren't much help. Azron bore a hunted expression, his eyes flitting about constantly, as though searching for escape. The recalcitrant thief had never been comfortable with authority figures, and now that he was in the immediate presence of the most authoritative figure on the planet, it was playing havoc with his nerves. Handen, too, was little help—his features looked drawn and distracted, and his lips moved gently and constantly, as though working on a complex mental problem. The only one of the four who didn't seem especially bothered by the situation was Xharon.

Bip turned back toward the Emperor and nearly panicked as he realized he was almost at the foot of the throne dais. He gulped and looked up into the hard, amused gaze of Argustin's ruler, taking in the beautifully woven robe and the gilded weaponry, the long, groomed hair, and the dark, hollow eyes. Under his thin silver crown, Draegul looked almost exactly like the statues Bip had seen scattered throughout Panthalus. Unlike the statues, though, the Emperor's face didn't bear the thousand-yard stare of contemplative nobility. In real life, Draegul grinned like something deep-down and deadly.

Remembering Riley's brief tutelage in etiquette, Bip bowed low, keeping his eyes on the floor until told to rise by the Emperor. His companions mimicked the bow, bending at the waist and keeping their eyes fixed on the carpet. They hung there in genuflection for what seemed like an age, waiting for Draegul to acknowledge them.

Then they waited some more.

Finally, Draegul spoke, his thin voice carrying well in the acoustics of the reception hall. "Rise, do."

The doomsayers straightened their backs. Bip blinked rapidly to dispel the dizziness as the blood rushed back down from his head. Draegul chuckled, a sound that was both melodic and broken.

"Well, well," he said, "if it isn't the traveler, the doomsayer who brings us dire warnings from an ancient race. Bip Plunkerton, I believe?"

Bip gave a short bow again.

The Emperor stared at him for a while before turning his attention to Azron.

"And the thief, Azron Bezron."

"That's Azron Bezron, Diamond Geezer (1st class)…Your Worship," interjected Azron.

"Indeed," said Draegul, his voice cold. "Interrupt me again, and I shall tear out your tongue and make you eat it," he added, almost as an afterthought.

Azron swallowed hard and gave a short bow.

Draegul focused his attention on Handen, dismissing the thief as though he had never existed. "Ah, Handen Strike. The great adventurer. The man who cannot die. I've been looking forward to meeting you most of all."

Handen looked up, shaken from deep thoughts. He gave a short bow and said nothing.

Finally, the Emperor looked down at Xharon. "And my darling eccentric niece, Xharon. What a joy it is to see your shining face once more in my court."

"Hallo, uncle," said the warrior princess.

"And still running around in your undergarments, I see. Fantastic."

"Actually, Uncle, they're—"

"Yes, very good, very good. Now, I have been told by that dear doddering duke, Riley, that you have something of incredible importance to tell me. Please, put an end to the agony of my curiosity. What's up?"

Bip cleared his throat. This was the moment he had been rehearsing for since he had first been sent from Kaneq. "My lord," he began. "I come bringing a warning of utmost importance, lo, of worldly consequence…verily."

Draegul began distractedly polishing his nails on his robe. "Go on."

"Erm… It has been made known to me, by the ancient knowledge of my people and the calculations of Professor Riley, that a weapon launched from a civilization in a distant cosmos will collide with Bersch in about five days, twelve hours, and fifty-or-so minutes. A weapon powerful enough to destroy the entire world."

In the silence that followed, Draegul locked his gaze on the young Kaneqian.

"And is that everything?" he said.

Bip was momentarily flabbergasted. He looked at his friends. Azron shrugged, his face reflecting Bip's confusion. Handen seemed not to have noticed, his thoughts still elsewhere. Finally, Bip turned back to the Emperor.

"Er...yes? I suppose. Did you want me to repeat it?"

"No. No, that's quite all right. Thank you for your concern, but this information was made apparent to me quite some time ago. The situation is under control."

Bip frowned in puzzlement. "But that's impossible!" he said.

The Emperor's eyes narrowed just a little. "One is not used to being contradicted in one's own palace," he said.

"Sorry, Your Worship, it's just that...I was under the impression that the world was ignorant of the upcoming disaster. I was sent to warn you all!"

"Then I'm afraid you've wasted your time," Draegul said simply.

"Well, if you already knew, then why didn't you tell anyone? Why did you send your men to try and stop us?"

The Emperor was silent for a moment. "You know," he began, his voice eerily calm, "I've had better men than you flayed alive for taking such a tone with me..."

Bip blanched in sudden terror.

"But since you are a stranger in these lands, I will give you the benefit of the doubt. The reason I have never made it public knowledge that the end of the world is approaching is because I do not wish to have panic on my streets. As you have no doubt seen on your way here, people tend to get a mite hysterical if they think they're all going to die soon."

Bip gulped, his mouth suddenly dry. Part of his mind was entertaining the idea that his entire journey, his mission, his quest, had been a giant waste of time. So far, the rest of his mind was quietly ignoring it.

The Emperor continued, "And I sought to apprehend you for no other reason than to stop you spreading fear across my Empire. Now, once again, thank you for your concern, but the situation is being looked into by the finest minds on Bersch. In other words, things are under control. You have wasted your time and you have wasted mine. You are dismissed."

Bip began to sway on the spot, his head spinning. "How could you have known? Some of the things I've learnt even Truggle didn't know about… How could you have known?"

"You are *dismissed!*" hissed Draegul. He clicked his fingers and suddenly various shadows around the reception hall revealed themselves to be Imperial guardsmen. They stood with the quiet menace of those eagerly awaiting the order to become extremely violent.

"Thank you, my lord," said Bip quietly. He turned around slowly, as if in a dream, and began walking toward the exit, conscious of the gaze of heavily armed men on the back of his neck. As he passed Handen, he looked up at the adventurer and paused. Gone was the faraway look of concerned contemplation, replaced instead by a fury Bip had never seen before. He stepped back in shock.

"Handen?"

The adventurer continued to stare ahead. If he had heard Bip, he made no attempt to acknowledge him.

"Handen? Come on—we've done all we can. It's time to leave."

Handen continued to stare straight ahead. He whispered something that Bip couldn't make out.

"Pardon?"

"Bastard."

Bip looked around wildly, trying to see what had so suddenly infuriated his friend. "Handen, I really think we should—"

"*Bastard!*" screamed the immortal, pointing an accusing finger at Draegul. The Emperor's eyes opened wide in shock. Around the room, there was a lethal sound of flintlock rifles being readied.

Azron stepped over and grabbed Handen's arm. "This isn't the time, mate. Let's just get out of here while the getting is good, yeah?"

Handen shook off the thief's grip and began advancing on the Emperor's throne.

"Stop right there, Mr. Strike," Draegul said, his manner cool. "Stop right there, or I'll have you cut down like a rotten tree."

The adventurer raised an accusing finger once more. "You!" he growled, rage bubbling in his words. "You were the one who had me locked up! You were the one who put me in prison for half a millennium!"

There was a silence around the hall that could have crushed worlds. A silence found beneath oceans and above stars. It was a sound that precluded the birth of universes, unbearably cacophonic in its sheer noiselessness.

"I beg your pardon?" said Draegul.

"Don't you dare play dumb with me," snapped Handen. "All this time I thought I'd failed in my mission, all this time I spent locked away in that blasted asylum—and you *knew*! You've always known. That's why you had me locked up!"

Draegul's eyes narrowed, his lip curling into a genteel sneer. "I'm afraid I have no idea what you're talking about."

Bip studied his friend's face, trying to fathom this unprecedented expression of sheer rage. "Handen? What do you mean?"

"That's why he knows what's going on," snarled Handen. "Because I told him hundreds of years ago."

Draegul chuckled. "What a comical mix-up—you must be mistaking me for one of my ancestors!"

Handen shook his head slowly and then, without warning, leapt at the Emperor. Several shots were fired, one striking Handen in the shoulder, but the immortal continued unhindered, grabbing at Draegul's robe and tearing it away from his chest.

"What do you think you're doing, you madman?" screeched the Emperor.

Two guardsmen leaped at Handen, restraining him, but it was too late. Handen struggled to free his arm, then pointed at the tattoo revealed on the Emperor's chest—a snake eating its own tail, twisted at the middle to form a figure of eight. Then, he tore away his own shirt to reveal the identical tattoo beneath.

"The mark of the immortal!" he shouted.

For a while, the Emperor and the adventurer stared at one another, locking gazes, neither blinking.

"Hang on a minute," said Xharon, breaking the tense silence. "Are you trying to tell me that Uncle Tommy's an immortal, like you?"

"Think about it," Handen said, keeping his eyes locked firmly on Draegul's. "The family resemblance, the fact that nobody ever sees his children, his successors. The fact that, throughout history, every Draegul bride has died young..."

Xharon gasped. "Auntie Yvette..."

"He's an immortal, ruling as Emperor of Argustin for a thousand years or more."

Draegul laughed, a dangerous and creeping laugh.

Handen continued, "When I warned him about the astral disaster centuries ago, he refused to take me seriously. I called him an arrogant fool, and he tried to have me executed. When he found out I couldn't die, he had me locked away forever."

"Is this true?" demanded Bip.

Draegul chuckled. "Oh dear, oh dear. And to think I was going to let you all go. Well, to be honest, I was going to have you all assassinated while you slept, but at least your deaths would have been quick. Now, I'm afraid, I shall have to dispose of you all as slowly and painfully as possible."

"What?" wailed Bip. "Why?"

"Because we know the truth," growled Handen. "The people might accept being ruled by a vicious psychotic tyrant, because that's the way it has always been, but if they find out that the reason it's always been that way is because they have, for centuries, been ruled by *the same* vicious psychotic tyrant, they might not remain so placid."

Draegul gave a small, sarcastic round of applause. "Very good, Mr. Strike."

"You had Auntie Yvette killed?" Xharon said, her bottom lip wobbling.

Draegul sighed. "Yes. It was a great shame. She was a lovely woman, but of course, she began to grow old. I couldn't have people becoming suspicious of me, so she had to die."

"You monster!" cried Xharon.

Draegul snapped his fingers. "Have her taken to the tower."

Instantly, a large group of Imperial guards appeared as if from nowhere, grabbing the warrior princess from all sides. She struggled, but to no avail.

"Unhand her!" roared Handen.

"Or what?" replied the Emperor. "As I'm sure you've noticed, I have you outgunned. You are unarmed, and while *you* may be impervious to death, I somehow doubt your friends are."

Handen gritted his teeth and clenched his fists, every fiber of his being crying out for action.

"Now," said Draegul. "I must say I'm very sorry, my dear, amusing niece. I never meant for you to become involved in all of this mess, but since you are, I'm afraid you can never see the light of day again. Ta-ta."

Xharon screamed in fury as she was half-dragged and half-carried away by the guardsmen.

Bip's mind reeled. Tears of helpless frustration rolled down his cheeks. "I don't understand! Handen was right; the world *really is* going to end. You know this!"

"Yes?" said Draegul.

"So why have him locked up? Why have any of us locked up?"

"I thought he made it quite clear. I don't appreciate being called a fool."

"But we might be able to help!"

Draegul laughed again, a sound that was dirty in his mouth. "What makes you think I need your help? I have already told you—the situation is well in hand. I have no need of 'ancient wisdom'—I *am* ancient wisdom!"

"Wisdom isn't acquired with time alone, Draegul," snarled Handen. "You're living proof of that."

The Emperor's smile faded instantly. "That's the second time you've insulted me, Mr. Strike, and it is the second time you will pay dearly."

"Oh dear…" muttered Azron.

"Look, you can't lock us up!" said Bip. "It's too late—your secret's out! All these guards now know you're an immortal! One of them is bound to talk!"

"Unlikely," said Draegul, smoothly, "since each and every one of my elite have their tongues cut out at birth."

"Oh…"

"Nice try, mate," muttered Azron.

"This isn't right!" cried Bip. "We were just trying to help! We never wanted to harm anybody! Please don't lock us away!"

"All right," said Draegul.

Bip blinked in surprise. "What?"

"I won't have you locked away."

Bip peered around at his comrades. "Really?"

"No. I thought I made it clear earlier. I'm going to have you killed horribly."

"No!"

Draegul rose to his feet and smiled a sinister smile. "Guards, have them fed to the bandersnatch."

"Oh dear, oh dear…" muttered Azron.

"And afterward, bring me the remains of Handen Strike." Draegul sneered down at the adventurer. "Your demise will not be so quick as your companions'. After you recover from your encounter with the bandersnatch, as you doubtless will, I will have you boiled alive in effluent for the rest of eternity."

"Well, it beats hanging around here and listening to you," snapped Handen.

Draegul's face darkened with fury. "Take them away. Feed them to the bandersnatch. We'll see how cocky you are when you're being digested alive."

The three remaining doomsayers backed up as they suddenly found themselves face-to-face with a dozen heavy flintlock rifles.

"You know," said Azron, "that could have gone a lot better."

The guards advanced.

"Wait!" bellowed Handen.

The Emperor raised a hand, and the guardsmen backed away from the adventurer.

"You have something to say?" he purred.

"Your problem is with me. These two can do you no harm—why not just let them go?" demanded Handen.

Draegul smiled. "And where would be the fun in that?"

"It's me you're angry with, me who insulted you all those years ago—it's me you want to punish!"

"And I have you. And as an added bonus, I have your friends as well. Tell me, why on Bersch would I give that up?" Draegul chuckled.

"Coward!" Handen shouted.

Draegul stood bolt upright, a dangerous glint in his eye. "Say that again, and I'll have you watch as my guards quarter your companions."

Handen sneered. "Yes, you have your guards to hide behind. It must be easy to make threats with your own army to back you up."

"Silence!" roared Draegul.

"I wonder if you know what true power is? I wonder if you've ever fought your own battles?"

"*Silence!*"

"Prove your worth! Back up those big words with some action! Your problem is with me, so fight me!"

Draegul stood stock still, staring at his prisoners.

Handen cracked a wry smile. "What have you got to lose? You can't die. Fight me."

"And if you win?"

"You let my friends go. You'll still have me."

"And if I win?"

"Then you get to go through the rest of your life knowing that you've beaten the best. All by yourself. Without hiding behind hired thugs."

Draegul laughed. "I suppose you expect me to back down so you can have some sort of tawdry moral victory to keep you feeling cozy over the countless years of agony I have in store for you? Well, I'm afraid that's not going to happen. You see, I've always had a love of weapons, and I've had a thousand years to get used to them. I *am* the best. And I shall enjoy proving it to you."

Draegul drew the ornate katana from the scabbard by his side. The blade shone like a phantom in the afternoon light.

"Guards. Give the fool a weapon and then make room."

"Oh dear, oh dear, oh dear…" muttered Azron.

A sword was placed into Handen's hand. He swung it experimentally. It was well-balanced and of sturdy craftsmanship but looked a clumsy affair in comparison to the Emperor's blade.

"Hold this," said Handen, passing his waterskin to Bip. Bip took it carefully, wary of the contents, and swung the strap over his shoulder.

Draegul, with a delicate flourish, moved swiftly into a ready stance. "I agree to your terms. If you can best me, your friends may go free. Now, be on your guard."

"I always am," Handen growled.

The combatants leaped toward one another, blades shining and singing through the air. They collided with a scream of steel, weapons locked together, fighters face-to-face.

"You know, I'm rather glad you had this idea, Mr. Strike," said Draegul, grinning through clenched teeth. "When I beat you, I may have your head mounted in my study."

"Then allow me to familiarize you with it in advance!" said Handen, and butted the Emperor on the nose. The swordsmen broke off, Draegul staggering backward but quickly recovering his guard.

On the sidelines of the fray, Azron nudged one of the guards. "One nil to us, aye?" he said.

The guard said nothing, merely eased the hammer back on his rifle with a heavy click.

"Ah," said Azron, suddenly aware that you didn't need a tongue if you were armed to the teeth. He focused his attention back on the fight.

The immortals circled one another, each judging the best angle of attack and defense. Suddenly Draegul lunged, an unexpected slash from his lower right quarter to his upper left. Handen dodged back, deflecting the blow…but only just.

Draegul grinned. "You know, it's amazing how much fun one can have living forever as the ruler of the civilized world, being able to do as one pleases for the rest of eternity. Wine, women, riches—every whim accounted for. I'm sure you'll appreciate that thought while you're rotting in whatever dungeon I decide to leave you in."

"You talk too much," said Handen. "Haven't you become tired of the sound of your own voice over the years?"

The adventurer lunged, a testing blow that forced Draegul back on his guard. Then he struck out three times from varying angles, each blow expertly deflected by the Emperor's blade. Draegul riposted with a wide arc from his sword, repelling Handen's assault and gaining back his ground.

Handen studied his opponent carefully, the world outside the fight no longer existing. Then he attacked, a flurry of fierce one-handed blows, advancing all the while as Draegul was forced back into a defensive posture. Just as it seemed the adventurer was getting the upper hand, Draegul struck another unexpected rising blow, this time catching Handen's cheek.

"First blood to me!" cried Draegul gleefully.

Handen touched his face, wincing as he felt the deep gash. With any luck, the wound would not swell up and impair his vision…but luck seemed to be avoiding him lately. He readied his guard, once again circling his opponent.

On the sidelines, Bip became aware that he had been holding his breath. He let it out in an urgent sigh. "Come on, Handen. Please, do this!" he whispered.

Handen waited for an attack, but to no avail. The Emperor was fighting defensively, confident enough of the speed of his blade to thwart Handen's blows, waiting for the mistake that would allow him to run his opponent through.

Draegul smiled a thin, lizard smile. "Is this the best our saviors from the stars have to offer? Is this their mightiest warrior?" The Emperor switched his grip on his katana, swirling the blade around him in a defensive weave. "I have to say, I'm very disappointed."

"I'm going to beat you," said Handen, his voice flat, calm, and deadly. "It's what I do."

With that, he attacked again—huge, sweeping blows that cleaved sparks from the Emperor's defending blade. He pressed his attack, awaiting the Emperor's inevitable riposte. It came in the form of another low blow, but this time one that Handen had anticipated. He brought his weapon down, trapping his opponent's katana against the stone floor. Then he stepped forward and rocketed a powerful kick into Draegul's solar plexus. The Emperor bent double, his face turning strained and purple, an uncontrolled groan erupting from his throat. Without hesitation, Handen swung his fist in a low arc, rising to an uppercut, the momentum of which lifted his feet from the ground. The Emperor somersaulted through the air, landing with a heavy thump.

"Yes!" shouted Bip. There was no doubt that Handen had won the match.

Draegul looked up, blood streaming from his mouth. His eyes crossed to take in the tip of Handen's sword, leveled unwaveringly at his throat.

"I believe I have bested you," said Handen. "Now for your part of the bargain."

Draegul smiled horribly through thick gore. "Certainly," he said, and raised his hand.

Without warning, a terrible boom reverberated throughout the hall as several dozen flintlocks were fired at once. Handen jerked spasmodically and was thrown to the floor, torn apart by bullets. He lay still on the ground, blood oozing from his multiple wounds, a puddle forming and expanding at a nauseating pace.

"No!" cried Bip, and ran to the body of his fallen friend.

Draegul stood up, wiping the blood from his mouth. He looked down at the unconscious Handen. "Fool," he muttered.

Bip looked up, tears in his eyes. "How could you?"

"He did not best me," snarled Draegul. "How could he? I am immortal! I am the Emperor of this land! He could *never* best me."

"But you gave your word!"

"Pah! I gave my word to a convicted madman. It means nothing. Guards!"

Guardsmen quickly surrounded the trio.

"Have them taken to the bandersnatch's lair. I do not wish to see them again."

Bip tried to fight the rising tide of despair in his belly as he, Azron, and the unconscious Handen were seized by the Imperial elite. "You gave your word!" he wailed.

Draegul said nothing, merely waved his hand as if to dismiss them.

The doomsayers were taken from the reception hall, and Draegul stood alone in silence. Soon he began to hear the whispers.

THEY WERE MANHANDLED into the bowels of Dawncastle, the seedy, crypt-like stonework of the lower levels an unwelcome contrast to the crystalline splendor of the levels above. Here was the reality of the great palace—here, with the dungeons and torture chambers, where the wails of the hopeless and the dying echoed horribly through the tight corridors and the torch light licked suggestively at deep and clawing shadows.

Handen groaned as he was dragged along. He was coming around, but the extent of his wounds meant that he was healing slowly. Azron watched with faint disgust as the immortal spat out a bullet.

"What is a bandersnatch, anyway?" said Bip, his voice oddly light and faraway-sounding to his heavily shocked mind.

"Well, it's not quite as big as a jabberwocky," said Azron. "Though it's definitely bigger than a jubjub bird, and much more vicious."

"Oh."

"It's pretty frumious too, by all accounts."

"Ah. Not good, then?"

"No. I imagine if it was small and docile, we wouldn't be getting fed to it, would we?"

"No, I suppose not."

The guards halted by a heavy-looking trapdoor. One of them began turning a crank that slid the doors across, slowly revealing a murky blackness beneath. There was a stench that reminded Bip suddenly of when he had been a boy and a rat had crawled under his bed and died. For a long time, he'd thought the smell had something to do with puberty until his mother had eventually found the real cause.

The trio were lined up, the gaping hole before them. One of the guards pointed down.

"I think they want us to go in," said Azron.

Bip peered into the blackness. "Erm… no. No, thanks. I'd rather not, if it's all the same to you." He swallowed deeply as he felt a flint-lock pressed into the back of his skull. "Oh. Okay, then."

Closing his eyes, the Kaneqian took a step forward into what was likely his doom.

———

FAR OUT INTO the cold drifts of space, the Massive Ball of Death felt the warmth of a new sun against what passed for its face. It had been a long time alone, nothing but the idle anticipation of arrival to keep it occupied, nothing but the pinpoint shine of distant stars to light its way. Now it knew for sure that it was merely days from its destination and, for a quasi-lifeform at the end of a journey measured in millennia, a few days was no time at all. It felt nervous, something new and exciting. It felt as though it had just arrived at a very important party and wasn't sure if it was dressed appropriately.

It gazed forward with what would pass for eyes, dimly aware that —for better or worse—it was nearing the end.

5

And Burbled As It Came...

Bip stood up and shivered, waiting for his eyes to adjust to the darkness. He wasn't sure how far he had slid, though the fall through the pitch-black tunnel had seemed like it had lasted an eternity. He heard a thump behind him.

"Bugger!"

"Azron? Is that you?" he whispered.

"Yes, it's me. Much as I wish it wasn't."

There was another thump followed by a groan.

"Handen? Is that you?"

"I think so. Where are we?"

"In the lair of a ferocious beast that needs feeding."

"Oh," said Handen bitterly. "Of course we are."

Bip peered around the lair. The shallow light filtering in through the trapdoor above was just enough that he could make out his surroundings. It was a natural cave, its walls slick with unnamed slime, the floor soft with something squishy, the origin of which Bip felt was best not guessed at. The whole cave stank of wild animal.

"Now what?" said Azron

Bip shrugged, a futile gesture in the dark.

"Handen?"

The adventurer groaned. "I've just been shot to death," he said. "It's going to be a little while yet before I'm much good for anything."

"Fair enough. We'll just sit here and be eaten then, shall we?"

"What are we up against?" Handen asked.

"A bandersnatch."

Handen sucked in his breath through his teeth. "Tricky," he said. "Are there any weapons lying around?"

"No."

"Any conveniently pointy pieces of wood or club-like hunks of rock?"

"No."

"Damn."

Now that his eyes were adjusting, Bip could make out a huge iron gate near the back of the cave. He felt his heart race as he heard the far-off echo of clanking gears. The gate began to open with a rusty yawn.

"This is it," he whispered.

"Spread out," said Handen. "Don't make us an easy target."

Azron's voice rang out from above them. "Way ahead of you, mate."

Bip looked up. By some fantastic feat of agility, Azron had managed to scramble up the cave wall, prying himself into the rock like a panicked cat.

"I'll be up here if you need me," he said.

"Great," said Bip, glumly. He turned to Handen, who was still slumped on the ground. He could see the adventurer now, and though he was still healing, he looked in no condition to fight.

"Any last-minute heroics in store?" Bip asked hopefully.

Handen shook his head. "Nothing comes to mind. Maybe I can let it eat me and hope it chokes to death..."

"Azron?"

"Can't think of anything, really. So far, the begin eaten thing is the best idea I've heard. Can't you do anything with that psyence of yours?"

Bip shook his head. "The only time that ever seems to work is by complete accident. And even then, it never works properly."

"Oh dear."

The gate was fully open now, revealing a total blackness behind it. The dark was split suddenly by two bright glows. There was a deep and sepulchral growl.

"Bandersnatch," Bip whispered.

The beast came forth, two sets of giant claws leading the way, followed by a larger set of teeth. The whole creature glistened with brown, reptilian skin and pushed its fat bulk along with spider-like legs that erupted from the crest of its spine. Its head was a misshapen thing, there only to give credence to its huge tunnel of a mouth. Two clear, wet orbs served as the creature's eyeballs, and a long, blue tongue flicked lazily from its jaws, sweeping the air before it like the cane of a blind man.

It burbled as it came.

"Well, chaps," said Azron. "It's been a blast, and I've had some good times, but I have to say, I wish I'd never met either of you."

"I'm starting to wish I'd never met me either," said Bip thickly, his tongue numb with terror.

The bandersnatch screeched like nails scraping on a blackboard and began shuffling slowly into the cave. Bip stared into the oblivion of its mouth, quite easily large enough to swallow him whole.

"So this is how it ends," he said, faintly.

"Cheer up," said Handen. "At least you did what you sent out to do. You warned the people that the end of the world was coming. It's all up to them now." The immortal chuckled softly. "And if this is how they repay you, maybe they deserve to be obliterated. Maybe Bersch was never supposed to be saved."

Bip's thoughts turned to Ted. Hadn't he said something similar? That Bersch being destroyed was all part of the order of things? If that was the case, why had Mr. Random been trying to stop him?

As if awaiting a cue, the world slowed down, the burble of the bandersnatch winding down to a low gurgle. A sensation of innate wrongness permeated the atmosphere.

"Hullo," said Mr. Random.

"Oh. You," said Bip.

Mr. Random's razor smile gleamed in the darkness. "Yes. Me."

"Well, I'd love to hang around and chat, but I'm a bit busy at the moment," said Bip, testily.

"Ah, yes. Your appointment with a certain and painful death."

"Yep. I don't suppose you had anything to do with this, did you?"

Mr. Random polished his long fingernails on his suit jacket. "Well, I might have whispered a certain something in a certain ear…"

"Well, that's just great. Thanks a lot."

"There's no need to be testy," said Mr. Random. "I just came to say goodbye. I'd like to think there are no hard feelings between us. Two players on opposing sides, the spirit of sportsmanship, etcetera, etcetera…"

Bip told him where he could stuff his sportsmanship.

"Well, there's no need to be like that," said Mr. Random. "I just came around to say hard luck, that's all."

"Yeah, you must be feeling very pleased with yourself. Now, thanks to you, this entire planet will be destroyed, and everything I've done will be for nothing."

Mr. Random blinked his yellow eyes, a puzzled smile on his face. "Pardon?"

"I said, thanks to you, Bersch is going to be destroyed!"

Mr. Random began to laugh, a low chuckle that quickly rose to a boyish giggle. "You don't know, do you? All this time trying to stop you, *and you don't even know!*"

"Know what?"

"Oh dear, oh dear, oh dear."

"Know what?"

"Well, I'm sorry, Bippy-boy, but I've got to dash. You know how it is—places to destroy, people to ruin."

"Know what?"

Mr. Random twiddled his long fingers. "Toodle-oo."

With that, he vanished, reality snapping back to normal around him.

Bip thought furiously. What had he meant? He felt that he had the pieces of an elaborate jigsaw puzzle and all that was left was to put them together. Would that he had the time...

The bandersnatch roared, closing in for the kill. Bip fled to the back of the cave, pressing his back against the walls. Azron scrambled farther still up the wall, and Handen crawled slowly away from the advancing beast.

Bip's mind raced furiously for any solution. *If only I had a weapon,* he thought. *Not that it would do much good, but it might make me feel better.* Suddenly inspiration hit him in a brilliant flash. He *did* have a weapon. He'd had a weapon all along! He reached down to the rotted waterskin at his side and uncorked the top of it.

He had one chance.

"Hey, you! Bandersnatch! Yeah, I'm talking to *you!*"

The beast swung its massive head in Bip's direction and opened its mouth to let loose a fearsome roar.

Bip tried to think of something disarmingly witty to say, but he couldn't. Instead, he just threw the waterskin into the mouth of the bandersnatch. There was a brief, puzzled silence as the monster swallowed. Then it belched massively and exploded.

Bip stood in stunned silence, bits of black goo from the exploded bandersnatch dripping from his clothes and hitting the floor with wet smacking sounds.

"What the hell happened there?" cried Azron, sliding down from the cave wall.

Bip had a thoughtful, faraway look in his eye. "I should have said, 'Open wide' or 'Fancy a drink?' Something like that, anyway."

Handen struggled to his feet. "How did you do it?"

Bip felt suddenly guilty. "I...I used the water from the fountain of death."

"All of it?"

"Yes. Sorry."

Handen stared for a while before slowly nodding his head. "It's fine. I can always go back to the dead wood," he said. "Hell, I've been alive for more years than I can remember. A few more months won't hurt."

"So that's what that water does, then," said Azron, wiping a chunk of gore from his cheek. "Pretty messy."

"Yep. So. Now what?"

"Some sort of daring escape?" suggested Handen. "That's what normally happens in these situations."

"A good idea, guv," said Azron. "Only how do we get out?"

Almost as soon as Azron had said this, there was a light thump. Behind them, a rope had been lowered from the trapdoor above.

"Hello down there?" came a voice. "Are you alive? By all that isn't deceased, are you *alive* down there?"

Handen smiled widely. "Professor DeChambre!" he called.

There was a distant sigh of relief. "When I heard what had happened, I came as soon as I could. I feared I might be too late!"

Bip looked back at the exploded carcass of the bandersnatch. "You're just in time," he called.

HANDEN WAS the last to shimmy up the rope, still too weak from his wounds to make use of his strength. Bip and Azron hauled him up over the edge of the trap door, and he lay panting for a while. Eventually, he looked up into Riley DeChambre's round face.

"My God, man, what did they do to you?" gasped the professor.

Handen grinned, a thin trickle of blood dripping from his mouth as he did so. "Nothing that I won't recover from," he said. He looked about. Thankfully this level of the dungeon was deserted. "How did you get past the guards?"

Riley held out a handheld device. It was boxy, bulky, and had various antennae, light bulbs, and small dials attached to it. It went *beep*. "A recently developed prototype of my own invention. It's a Dimensional Oscillatron and Frequency Energy Recalibrater."

Azron blinked. "A Do-fer?"

The professor looked critically at his device. "Yes. Yes, I suppose you could call it that."

"And what does it do, exactly?"

"Well, it recalibrates the energy frequency of dimensional oscillations."

"Come again?" said Azron.

"In a nutshell, it allows you to control your position in space/time by observing the frequencies of certain dimensional signals and manipulating them with modified frequencies of your own, effectively allowing you to hack into energy megarhythms in a subspace dimension and alter them in conjunction with your own specific biofrequencies to suit your purposes. In this case, it allowed me to transport instantaneously from my workshop to this location without, as it were, going through the front door."

"Sounds complex," said Bip.

"Yes, it is, rather," conceded Riley.

"Some kind of teleportation device?" offered Handen.

"In a way..." began Riley.

"You can explain it to me later," Handen interrupted. "Can we use it to get out?"

"Certainly."

"Then let's do that."

"Erm... Aren't we forgetting someone?" said Bip.

"Of course. Xharon," said Handen. "She's being held in the tower. Damn!"

Riley shook his head mournfully. "There must be a hundred guards between us and the tower. I could attempt to reconfigure the... the Do-fer...but it would take some time."

"It's too dangerous to be hanging around here longer than we have to," said Azron.

"And we don't have any weapons," Handen added.

"Ah," said Riley brightly. "I did take the liberty of bringing a few supplies with me." He emptied a bag onto the floor, the contents of which clanged noisily. There was an assortment of weaponry, including Brian and Xharon's axes. "It pays to be prepared. By all that's precautionary, *it pays to be prepared.*"

"It certainly does," said Handen, grinning menacingly as he took two weapons from the pile. They were the prototype pistolas from DeChambre's workshop. "You know, I feel better already," he said.

"So what's the plan?" said Azron.

Handen spun the revolving ammunition chamber on each pistola in turn. "Simple, really," he said. "We take on the guards, get the girl, and somewhere along the line, an explosion chases us down a corridor."

Azron and Bip exchanged an uncertain look.

"Trust me," said Handen. "This is what I do."

AS HE CHARGED, there was a dual click from his pistolas—he had run out of ammunition. He threw the weapons aside and, bellowing all the while, continued to assault what was left of the contingent. As the two remaining guardsmen feverishly reloaded their heavy rifles, he leapt into the air, twisting like a salmon, and brought his heels down on the helmet of the foremost guard with a low *crunch*. The guardsman crumpled to the floor like a marionette whose strings had just been cut.

The remaining guardsman, having no time to reload his rifle, threw the now-useless weapon aside and drew a huge two-handed broadsword from the scabbard at his side. The attacker smiled, drawing his blade with a casual flourish. The duel was quick and desperate, but it wasn't long before the guard fell, clutching at his guts.

Breathing hard, Handen checked his pocket watch. They were making good time.

"Clear!" he shouted.

Bip, Riley, and Azron appeared from around the corner, taking in the immediate aftermath of extreme violence.

"Well done," said Azron. "Erm... Keep up the good work."

The sound of various alarm bells ringing in the distance was a continuous aural litany. The guardsmen of Dawncastle were well aware of the prisoners' escape, and the glass palace was raging with the sound of clanking armor and weapons being readied.

Handen had been fighting like never before, reveling in the chaos of unleashed combat. He was still not fully recovered from his wounds, and now had a few fresh ones to add to his collection, but he had been operating on sheer adrenaline, taking on everyone who had stood in their way.

He checked the remaining ammunition for his pistolas. Three bullets left, then it would all be down to swords and luck.

"How close are we?" he said.

"If memory serves, the door to the tower should be at the end of this corridor," said Riley.

"Then let's go."

They burst through the door into the tower beyond. There was a spiral staircase that seemed to go on forever. They ran until their lungs burned and their legs went weak, then they were at the top, another corridor and another heavy-looking door barring their way.

"Stand back!" roared Handen. He fired a pistola three times at the door's lock, then gave it an almighty kick. The door flung open, and the escapees ran through, ready for any possible danger. What they hadn't been ready for was absolutely no danger at all. Beyond the doorway was a comfortable room with a cozy-looking fireplace and a four-poster bed. The walls were lined with bookshelves, on which rested hundreds of tomes. In the center of the room, a long and laden dining table held the remnants of a feast. Xharon sat at the head of the table, a look of guilty surprise on her face and a napkin tucked into her collar.

"What the hell are you doing here?" she cried.

Bip frowned. "Rescuing you?" he offered.

Xharon stood bolt upright. "Now let's get one thing straight—I'm a warrior princess, and I don't get rescued! I *do* the rescuing! As a matter of fact, I was bally well on my way to rescue you!"

Handen surveyed the luxurious prison cell. "What kept you?"

Xharon took the stained napkin from her collar and discarded it as though it had never been there. "I was just waiting for the guards to bring the second course," she said. "So I could overpower them… You know."

Azron interrupted. "Look, I hate to be a bore and everything, but I hear guards. Lots of guards. Now might be a good time to skedaddle."

Handen went to the door. In the distance but getting closer, he could hear the heavy tramp of booted feet.

"We have to get out of here. Professor, do you think you could reconfigure the… the…"

"The Do-fer?" said Azron, helpfully.

"Yeah, that."

Riley looked up from the bizarre machine, which was currently emitting a low whirring noise. "I'm already on it. By all that's dynamic, I'm already *working on it*. I'll just need a few minutes."

Handen looked down the corridor. The shouting and the clanking of armor was getting closer. "We may not *have* a few minutes," he said.

"Wait a minute!" demanded Xharon. "What exactly is going on here?"

"We're getting out," replied Bip.

"Oh, no you don't," said Xharon. "I told you. I'm not going to be rescued like some helpless damsel. It's not my style."

Bip sighed wearily, then reached into Riley's bag. He pulled out Xharon's axes and offered them to her. "How about you think of it as assisting us with our escape?"

Xharon took the axes and weighed them thoughtfully. "Yes. Yes, that sounds more like me. Okay, let's do it!"

They went out into the corridor where the shadows of the advancing guards could be seen ascending the spiral staircase. Bip drew Brian, holding it in the defensive stance he had been taught so long ago. Xharon began twirling her axes in a complex streak of metal. Azron splayed his limbs, ready to duck and dive.

"Right," said Handen. "I suppose this is where we find out what we're made of."

Azron gulped. "I'd rather leave that a comfortable mystery if it's all the same to you," he said.

"Just a few more minutes and it should be fine," said Riley, with annoying chirpiness.

Handen drew his bastard sword as the Imperial guardsmen came into sight. There were a dozen of them, some armed with rifles, some with an impressive and lethal-looking array of heavy blades.

"Won't be a moment," said Riley. Behind them the buzzing sound grew in intensity, harmonized by a high-pitched whistle.

The guardsmen armed with rifles took on a firing formation, while the swordsmen flanked the corridor, advancing all the while. Handen recognized the formation—they were going to be driven into the center of the corridor by the swordsmen, then cut down by rifle fire. He breathed hard, prepared to go down fighting.

Bip gripped his weapon, uncomfortably aware that they were trapped and outnumbered. Worse still, he wondered if he would even be able to use the blade—he still wasn't comfortable with the idea of fighting or killing. He looked over at Xharon, who, despite the odds against them, was grinning confidently. He wondered if he'd ever understand her.

"Not long now. By all that's immediate, *we haven't long!*"

The buzzing sound increased; the whistling gave way to a low hum that ascended with electric fury. Ahead of them, the guards readied their rifles, the order to fire was given, and a split second later, there was the terrible flash of ignited powder.

Bip closed his eyes as the machine reached a filthy crescendo of noise.

He opened his eyes. The world was how it had been, except still and distant, as though he were viewing it from under water. He crossed his eyes at the bullet that was advancing, with snail-pace slowness, toward his nose. He tried to open his mouth to remark on this odd phenomenon, but couldn't. Then, delicately sketched with a thousand thin lines of darkness, the world began to waver, and finally disappeared.

Bip felt the uncomfortable nagging sensation of the dimensional traveler, that he was everywhere at once. It felt as though every cell in his body had gone cock-eyed or as though a billion people were whispering in his ear at the same time. He had a brief moment to reflect that he felt not just weightless, but massless, as though he were nothing at all. He opened his mouth to scream and scream and scream, but here, in these corridors of the universes, these dimensionless crawlspaces of anti-stuff, there was nothing to scream at.

There was nothing...and then there was the workshop.

"Ooorghk?" said Bip.

"Errink!" agreed Azron.

The room spun wildly, like a hard night's drinking catching up all at once. Bip fought the urge to vomit and closed his eyes until the swaying stopped.

"What...was...that?" he panted.

Professor DeChambre seemed mostly unaffected by the transition. In fact, he still seemed quite chirpy. "That, my young friend, was the sensation of temporarily being unfixed to a specific dimension. I call it 'Transgressing Immediate Reality-lag.'"

Azron groaned. "Thank you. I feel so much better now that I know what it's called."

Xharon burped in seasick kind of way. "It's horrible," she moaned.

Riley shrugged. "Well, I suppose you get used to it."

Handen looked around the workshop. "We made it, then. We escaped. Well done, Professor."

Riley blushed. "It was nothing, really."

"Hang on a minute," said Bip. "What do you mean 'transgressing immediate reality'?"

Riley cleared his throat. "Well, it's quite straightforward, really—"

"I bet it's not..." mumbled Azron.

"*Quite straightforward.* We, each of us, perceive only a small number of the dimensions we exist in, and those we do not exist in, even though they may, in theory, constantly surround us, we may never experience at all. The reason that we, as dimensional residents, don't all bleed into the wrong dimensions is because of a sort of universal surface tension, a sort of static field that entraps specific and, theoretically, *relevant* frequencies. By disrupting our own frequencies in the immediate perceivable dimension—in this particular incidence, space/time—we were able to momentarily separate ourselves from that particular 'surface tension' and reposition ourselves in the space/time dimension by traveling through a subspace plane—effectively 'lifting off' and 'touching down' in a different part of the same dimension. While we are free-floating, as I like to call it, the entire dimensional frequency range is available for reading through the Do-fer; then it's just a simple matter of finding the desired part of the desired frequency and 'receiving' ourselves into it..."

The doomsayers stared with equally glazed eyes.

Riley faltered. "Umm... We were moving outside dimensional space. Think of it as a secret passageway, by all that's mysterious, or a shortcut between different places. A way to get from A to D without necessarily passing B and C."

Azron stared owlishly. "So...magic, then?"

Riley flustered. "Well, no—"

"Magic it is, then!" said Azron, clapping his hands together with an air of finality. "Why didn't you just say so?"

Riley opened his mouth to argue. Handen interrupted him.

"The fact is, it worked, and we're all safe. For now."

Bip sighed. "I suppose it's only a matter of time before the Emperor comes looking for us, yes?"

"Yes."

"So we'll have to go on the run again, yes?"

"Yes."

The Kaneqian sighed heavily again. "I was so looking forward to staying in the same place for a few days."

"Cheer up, guv," said Azron. "You could have been spending the rest of your short life being eaten by a monster."

Bip considered the point. It did not brighten his mood.

"But what about the astral disaster?" said Xharon. "Shouldn't we be trying to do something?"

Handen gave a noncommittal shrug. "I hate to say it, but the ball is in Draegul's court now. If I'm right, he's had a thousand or so years to think of a way to protect Bersch. If he hasn't come up with something by now, he never will. Our work here is done."

"Then why doesn't it feel as though we've won?" said Xharon.

Handen grinned. "It's not about winning, Xharon. It's about saving the world, which we've done everything in our power to do. It's up to Draegul now—he's the only one with the resources to blow this nuclear meteor out of the sky, right, Professor?"

Riley, who had been tinkering absent-mindedly with the Do-fer, looked up. "Oh, yes," he said. "If anyone could create a weapon large enough, it's Draegul. He has the money and know-how, and he has certainly had the time to work on the problem."

Xharon sighed in frustration. "It still doesn't feel right. What do you think, Bip?"

The princess waited for an answer. There wasn't one.

"Bip?"

Bip was staring into space, a look of abject horror in his eyes.

"What's the matter?"

The Kaneqian had been thinking—thinking about Mr. Random and his conversations with Ted, and suddenly it had hit him. "Professor?" he said, his voice barely more than a murmur.

"Yes?"

"How powerful would a weapon have to be to safely destroy a cluster of death-bombs roughly the size of the moon?"

Riley frowned. "Well, I suppose the only safe way to destroy it would be to completely vaporize it. A weapon of that magnitude would have to be very powerful indeed. Powerful enough to crack the world if they're not careful, I'll warrant."

"Powerful enough to shoot the stars from the sky?"

Riley laughed. "Well, I doubt anyone would go as far as to make a weapon *that* powerful. It would be ludicrous. Only a madman would..." The professor paused, a look of horrific realization overtaking his face.

"We were never supposed to stop the astral disaster," whispered Bip.

"What do you mean?" demanded Handen.

"The astral disaster was never the real threat. The astral disaster was the cure, not the condition. The real threat was an immortal all-powerful megalomaniac psychopath with the means to blow up worlds!"

Handen stared hard at the Kaneqian. "How do you know this?"

"It's the Discordance," breathed Bip. "Draegul is under the direct influence of the Discordance. For a thousand years he has been. They don't want to destroy just one planet—they want to destroy hundreds!"

Handen's eyes widened. "Of course! A trigger-happy idiot with a gun that big could unwittingly kick-start an interstellar war! It's not the world we have to worry about saving—it's the entire goddamned galaxy!"

Xharon's eyes lit up, and a dangerous smile curved her lips. "Brilliant!"

6

What Now?

Thousands of miles away, in the uncharted heart of Ghulbra Forest, the fifty-third centurial meeting of "Immortals Anonymous" was well under way.

The meetings had, of course, been Tanya's idea. It was intended as a way for people facing the emotional problems born of immortality to meet up with others in the same situation, share their burdens, and generally have a bit of a natter. She had called it a "support group," and immortals attended from all over the world, though mainly as a way to relieve their stupendous boredom rather than to derive any comfort the meetings might offer.

The IA meetings were unfailingly formulaic. They began with the group members sitting in a circle and talking about their respective problems and how they coped with them. Then they did a series of positive-thinking and group trust exercises—again, Tanya's idea—until finally they opened a bottle of wine, and a few more bottles of wine, until the meeting was called to an end with the entire group ceremoniously urinating into the fountain of youth.

Tanya had really made an effort this year, decorating the small cave-like dwelling with several hundred doilies and doily-esque fabrications. It took a very long time to fabricate a decent doily in the middle of the ancient forest with no access to any kind of the usual materials, but Tanya had had plenty of time on her hands and made a serviceable effort with weeds and bits of bark.

So now, surrounded by fervently organic doilies, Immortals Anonymous sat in a circle, linking hands and chanting one of the various chants Tanya had made up in her considerable spare time.

"Living forever, coping together! Living forever, coping together!"

The chant finished as it always did, with each participant stopping whenever the embarrassment became too much to bear, falling silent like a domino rally of anti-crescendo until only Tanya was left, chanting by herself until everybody started to feel really uncomfortable.

"Right, then!" she said, after she had finished her solo chant. "Who wants to start?"

The immortals looked at each other. No one wanted to start.

"How about you, Dathbert?" she said, singling out a young and bookish-looking man. "You're fairly new to the group—why don't you start us all off by telling us a bit about yourself?"

Dathbert winced. Tanya's condescending chirpiness brought back uncomfortable recollections of boarding school and campground activities coordinators. He stood up and cleared his throat. "My name is Dathbert, and I am an immortal."

"Hallo, Dathbert," the group chorused with all the enthusiasm of a funeral dirge.

Dathbert continued. "It's been five hundred years since I first drank from the fountain—"

"Pah!" interrupted one of the immortals. His name was Cully, and he had had the misfortune to drink from the fountain of youth when he was a very old man, believing that the fountain would reverse the ageing process rather than just halting it. Consequently, due to what he perceived to be a flagrant case of false advertising, he had run through the previous few millennia in a body racked with arthritis and an unstable digestive system. Justifiably, he was a very cranky old man.

Dathbert continued, unfazed by the interruption. "As I was saying, it's been five hundred years. I've done a bit of traveling, a lot of thinking—you know. Generally I've just been taking it one day at a time."

Dathbert sat down to half-hearted applause led by Tanya.

"Smashing, Dathbert, really. You're amongst friends, you know—you can cry if you want to."

"I don't want to cry."

"Don't feel you have to bottle it up—let it all out if you want."

"I don't want to cry."

"Because we're here for you, you know that, don't you?"

"God damn it, I don't want to cry!"

Tanya smiled. If she was in anyway offended by Dathbert's tone, she didn't let it show. "I think we can all learn from Dathbert's strength and wisdom," she said, nodding in what she thought was a deep and understanding way.

"Strength? Wisdom?" screeched Cully. "What's so wise about taking it one day at a time? What else *can* you do, really?"

There was a murmur of approval from the group.

"I bin' taking it one day at a time for nigh on three thousand years, and it ain't done me no good!"

The group murmured again.

Tanya smiled a patient smile. "Please, Cully—if you want to talk, you have to raise your hand first."

"Don't tell me to raise my hand, you young snipper! I've lived more lives than most can dream! I've seen things you people wouldn't believe! Attack ships on fire off the coast of Arglebaya! Torch-light glittering in the dark near the gates of Nebbela..."

Dathbert sighed. The speech was a familiar one. "And all these moments will be lost in time?" he offered.

"Yer' damn right!" screeched Cully. "Lost in time like... like...like a fart in a whirlwind."

"If you're quite finished!" said Tanya, frowning and putting her hands on her hips, her patience finally having reached its end. "Look, what's the point of a bloody support group if we're not going to bloody support each other?"

Cully shrugged. "Frankly, I don't see why we should *bother* supportin' each other. I mean, it's not as if we can go home and kill ourselves, is it? More's the pity…"

"Well, that's not strictly true…" interrupted another immortal. Her name was Margo, and being a Woman of a Certain Age for a practical eternity hadn't done much good for her positive outlook. "Look at Longbert."

Cully frowned and glanced around the assembled immortals. "Where is ol' Longbert?" he said.

"Well, that's just it," said Margo. "He isn't here; he's buried himself alive. He said he was just going to lie down and be quiet until his body took the hint and died."

Cully rolled his eyes thoughtfully. "That's not a bad idea."

Tanya gaped in horror. "Shouldn't we go and dig him up?" she cried.

"Are you kidding?" said Margo. "He'd be furious!"

Cully chuckled. "Good 'ol Longbert."

Tanya's temper frayed again. "Well, if that's your attitude, why do you lot bother to come here at all?"

"Bored."

"Boredom."

"Just bored, really."

Tanya looked about, her shoulders slumping as the anger slowly faded from her eyes. "I'll just open the wine then, shall I?"

The suggestion was met by enthusiastic approval.

"And then we can go and pee in that bloody fountain," added Cully.

There was a patter of genuine spontaneous applause, something that rarely happened at the IA meetings.

"SO WHAT NOW?" said Azron.

It was a fair question. It was a *good* question. The trouble was, it wasn't a particularly helpful one.

The doomsayers sat about the workshop, each of them toiling with their own thoughts.

"We could just kill him…if he wasn't an immortal," said Handen.

"And if he wasn't surrounded by his own personal army," added Azron.

Handen nodded distractedly.

"Why don't we just tell everybody? Tell the people?" said Xharon. "I'm sure if the word got around, there'd be some sort of uprising, wouldn't you say?"

Handen shook his head. "We hardly have the time to manufacture a rebellion, and besides, would people want to listen? What do they care if their leader starts taking pot shots at outer space? And who would have the nerve to stand up to him if they did?"

The group nodded its agreement. Draegul was feared by all, and with good reason.

"If I may interject, I think that sabotaging the weapon may be the most prudent course of action," said Riley, looking up from the device he was fiddling with.

Handen nodded again. "A good plan, with only two faults. One, we don't know where the weapon is or what it looks like, and two, we would still need it to avert the astral disaster."

"We could fire it ourselves then destroy it afterward?" suggested Xharon.

"We could," said Handen, "but we'd still have to find it. Professor, do you have any clue as to where this weapon might be hidden?"

Riley shook his head. "The information would be extremely classified, of that I've no doubt."

Bip raised his head. "Surely a plot to build an instrument designed to avert a world-destroying disaster would have caused some sort of stir? I mean, it doesn't seem like something you could keep a secret for very long."

Professor DeChambre shrugged. "For all we know, the instrument could be the size of a potato and Draegul puts it under his pillow at night."

"Are you sure you haven't heard anything at the palace, Professor?"

Riley shook his head. "There have been whisperings about something called Operation Deadwaker, but from what I can gather, it's some sort of archaeological project, by all that's immaterial."

"Damn," muttered Handen. "If only there was some way we could find out what Draegul has been working on."

"There *is* his study," said Riley. "He keeps detailed files of his projects there, or so I've heard."

"Excellent!" snapped Handen. "Where is his study?"

"Back at Dawncastle."

"Damn."

Bip sighed. "There's no way we could get back into Dawncastle. Not unless we had some sort of..." Bip paused and looked at the Do-fer. "We could use the professor's device!" he said. "Just dimension hop in and out again without anyone being the wiser!"

Professor DeChambre nodded. "You could certainly use it to get into Dawncastle; after all, I have the co-ordinate frequencies committed to the Do-fer's memory. Alas, though, I would not be able to pinpoint the exact location frequency of the study, or even the relevant floor. It would be far too specific. The only way would be to actually go into the study, record the frequency, then come back here, which, since no one may enter Draegul's study and we won't be able to get into Dawncastle without being killed, would be impossible."

"But we *could* get into Dawncastle?" asked Bip.

"Oh yes, by all that's easy-peasy—it would be a doddle."

"Well there we go, then!" cried Bip. "All we need to do is get into Dawncastle, break into the study, and steal Draegul's files!"

"You make it sound very simple," said Handen doubtfully.

"And it will be! At least it will be to a master thief!"

The group turned to look at Azron. He had been absentmindedly rolling a cigarette throughout the entire discussion. "What?" he said.

"I was just saying," said Bip, "that sneaking through Dawncastle and into a heavily secured room would be no problem for a genuine Diamond Geezer (1st Class) of the Port Town Union of Dodgy Fellows!"

Azron paled. "Oh, right," he said. "Yeah, well, normally that wouldn't be a problem at all, no worries, but right now I'm...erm...on a break, see?"

Handen frowned. "The fate of the world hangs in the balance and you're on a break?"

Azron shrugged and rolled his eyes. "Union rules," he said. "What can you do?"

"Come on, Azron," Bip said. "Stop mucking about. This is *serious!*"

Azron sighed heavily. "You're right, this is serious," he said. He took a deep breath then slowly let it out. "The truth is, I'm not a Diamond Geezer (1st Class). I'm not even a tin-badge thugling."

"What?"

"I lied. I never even made it into the Union—they disqualified me because I forgot to steal the pencil after I filled in my application form."

"But what about your certificate?" cried Bip.

"Not mine," said Azron miserably. "I stole it off some geezer and pasted my own details onto it."

"So you're not a master thief, then?" asked Handen.

"I'm not a master *anything*, mate," said Azron. "Except maybe a master cock-up."

Bip tutted under his breath. "I'm really disappointed in you, Azron. All this time I thought you were a sneaky, conniving deviant with the morals of an insect, and it turns out that you were lying all along."

"Yeah, well, now you know. And that's why I can't go into Dawncastle."

"Wait a minute," said Xharon. "Didn't you say that you stole that certificate?"

"Yeah?"

"It wasn't just lying around and you picked it up?"

"Heck, no," said Azron, crossly. "Give me *some* credit. I took it out of his house, didn't I?"

"And whereabouts did he keep this certificate?"

"The same place any good thief would keep it," said Azron, as though it were obvious. "In his socks."

"What, in his sock drawer?"

"Nah, in the socks he was wearing!"

Xharon grinned and shook her head. "Are you telling me that you stole a treasured possession from a master thief, from inside his socks, no less, and that doesn't entitle you to call yourself a Diamond Geezer of any class?"

Azron frowned. "Never thought of it like that," he muttered.

"Yes," said Bip, "and what about all the things you've stolen from *us* that we didn't know about?"

Azron shifted his gaze nervously about. "I didn't think you realized," he said.

"I didn't, really," said Bip. "I just assumed."

"Oh. Fair enough."

"So, how about it?" said Handen.

Azron looked up questioningly.

"Why don't you prove to us and to the world that you don't need a union or a certificate? Why don't you prove that you can be a master thief on your own terms?"

Azron stood up and straightened his long coat. "I'll need some things," he said.

Bip grinned and clapped him on the back. "I knew you wouldn't let us down!"

The tall thief smiled a sly smile. "Steady on, guv—how do you know I'm not going to just take all your stuff and run away?"

Bip's grin dropped.

"Just kidding," said Azron. "Stealing directly from the Emperor? I'll be a legend, mate, *a legend!* Those union chumps'll *eat* their stupid application form!"

CELIA DOOM BREATHED hot air into her hands and rubbed them together vigorously. It was a cold evening, and the red robes of the Cult of the Doomsayer didn't offer much in the way of insulation. She looked at the silhouette of Dawncastle, framed through the bars of the outer wall's high and ornately spiked gates. Without the sunlight,

Dawncastle relied on its internal lighting for illumination, and the building pulsed dimly with the glow of a thousand electric lights. Celia looked up at the night sky, free of clouds and chilly with starlight. Though the moon was bright and gibbous, it was upstaged by the silvery shine of the new star, the harbinger of destruction that the astrologers had named Tracy.

Celia sighed and turned back to the rest of the doomsayers. There weren't that many left. After all, the purpose of the Cult of the Doomsayer had been to warn the people of the impending end of the world. Now that the end of the world was here, it seemed a bit pointless to warn people about it.

"Right," said Celia. "Does everybody know why we're here?"

A cultist put up his hand. His name was Nigel, and he was a professional cultist, having previously been a long-serving member of both the Suicide Cult of Hope and Wisdom and the Deathbringer Cult of Peace and Love. He was very keen, and annoying with it.

Celia sighed. "Yes, Nigel?"

"*I* don't know why we're here."

The rest of the cultists groaned, and Celia rolled her eyes skyward. "All right, for the benefit of Nigel, I'll go through it one last time. Pay attention, Nigel. The Prophet of the Ancient Ones has asked me personally to cause a distracting disturbance at this gate in precisely five minutes. Okay?"

Nigel raised his hand again. Celia sighed. "Yes, Nigel?"

"But *why*? I mean, everybody knows it's the end of the world, but everything's under control—Emperor Draegul said so himself! That's why he let us out of jail, isn't it? Because we were right, and he was very grateful for our help?"

Celia raised a hand to her eyes. Nigel was right, of course, but that wasn't the point.

"Look, Nigel, what's the point of being in a doomsday cult if you're just going to stop when someone tells you that everything's fine? We're in it for the *long haul,* people, so let's get our act together! The Prophet has endowed us with a mission, and we will carry out his will to the bitter end! Verily!"

The cultists cheered. *This* was the sort of unthinking and blind zeal that you signed up to a cult for.

"Right!" roared Celia. "All together, now!"

The group drew in a collective breath, each recalling the chant they had rehearsed earlier in the day.

"Two, four, six, eight! We will wait outside your gate!"

"Six, seven, eight, nine! Right until the end of time!"

As one, the cultists looked up at the silver star in the sky, fat and twinkling and growing a little bigger all the time.

"Which should only be a couple of days, really, when you think about it!"

It wasn't long before a Regulator sidled toward the group. He was new to the job, just out of training, hence the fact that he sidled rather than marched and asked questions first rather than shooting.

He cleared his throat and, in a way that rookies are wont to do, recalled confrontational protocol to the letter.

"Ello, 'ello, 'ello. What's all this, then?"

Celia left the other cultists to chant on their own.

"It's a protest," she explained.

The rookie frowned. "What are you protesting against?"

Celia shrugged. "This and that."

"This and that? A bit vague, isn't it?"

"Yeah, well, we're cultists, aren't we? We're not renowned for our clarity of purpose…"

"I resent that!" called Nigel. "I'll have you know that I've been in plenty of cults with a very distinct clarity of purpose!"

Celia rolled her eyes and winked at the Regulator. "You see what I have to put up with? Don't let anyone tell you that being the leader of a cult is easy."

The Regulator blinked in puzzlement. Somehow he'd envisioned the confrontation taking quite a different route to what it was now.

Celia turned her full attention on Nigel. "Oh, yeah? And what was so distinctive about that suicide cult you were in, then?"

"It was our firm belief that the only way to achieve worldwide peace was if everybody killed themselves so their souls could be taken into the mothership and flown to a utopia in space, of course."

"Oh? And how come *you* didn't kill yourself, then?"

Nigel shuffled his feet. "I was ill that day."

"Too ill to kill yourself?"

"Yes. Very bad cold."

Celia put her hands on her hips. "Call yourself a cultist? You listen to me, Nigel; I've had more bizarre visions and spouted more prophecies than most sane people could even think of in a lifetime! I've verily'd and lo'd 'til my face exploded, and what have you done, eh? You sat in your stupid suicide cult and took a day off for the grand finale! So don't come the clever bugger with me, all right? Or I'll pull off your nose and shove it up a cat's bum! Right?"

"Yes, miss."

"That's better."

Celia turned back to the Regulator and smiled sweetly. "Now then, officer, was there something I could help you with?"

The rookie considered his options. He was on his own, surrounded by people who were quite definitely mad. He knew that the protocol called for him to signal for backup, but frankly he didn't like to think of what might happen before they arrived. He was fond of cats...but not that fond. It was then that he made a decision that would come more easily the more experience he gained in life. He decided to sod the protocol and make a run for it.

Celia watched him leave. "I wonder what he wanted?" she muttered, and turned back to the chanting.

"*Two, four, six, eight! We will stand outside your gate!*"

"*Six, seven, eight, nine! Chanting annoying numerical rhymes!*"

Celia watched as the bright searchlights atop Dawncastle's inner walls began to swing toward the protestors. The distraction was working.

AZRON LIT A CIGARETTE. It was a difficult thing to do when you were hanging upside down by your knees, but he did it anyway. He took a few puffs and had a bit of a think. The Do-fer had worked like a charm, transporting him to just outside the gates of Dawncastle. There had been a moment of blind panic while he had searched for a convenient shadow to conceal himself in, but once he'd found the darkness, he might as well have been invisible.

He was a champion lurker, so that was what he did for a while—he lurked, looking about and assessing the situation until Dawncastle's searchlights had swung toward a disturbance at the main gate. Acknowledging his cue, Azron had pulled the rope and grapnel from under his long coat and swung it soundlessly into the air above him. The grapnel had been coated with heavy rubber, so much so that he'd hardly heard it as it connected with the support girder above him. He'd shimmied up the rope and balanced on the girder, pulling the rest of the rope up behind him, then repeated the action until the guards and walls below him were far away, hushed and hidden from his higher perspective.

As the thief had scaled farther and farther up the palace walls, the grapnel had eventually become useless; most of the supports he had relied on for purchase had become too narrow at the tapering tip of the tower. He had coiled the rope and replaced it under his long coat, pulling out, instead, four rubber suction cups, which he attached to his knees and hands. Then, like a spindly spider in the night, he had crawled up the glass panels of Dawncastle, making soft *schluppschlupp* noises in the still air.

IN THE UPPER levels of Dawncastle, Maggot finally made his way to bed. It had been an eventful day, and he was glad to get back to his quarters. Tomorrow would begin another terrifying schedule of staying one step ahead of the mad Emperor. He poured himself a large shot of whisky, drank it in a single gulp, and stared out of the night-darkened window at the distant lights of the city. He caught the eye of his reflection and took in the long white beard and receding hairline. He had aged badly since becoming head of Whimstaff. To think he had only been twenty-eight when he had first signed on for the post...

Maggot froze suddenly. His reflection, old and tired as it was, seemed to change, becoming momentarily sharper and more sinister. Maggot squinted his eyes shut and opened them again. His reflection was once again looking its old tired self.

"I'm finally going mad," muttered Maggot. "Thank goodness. Maybe they'll take me away to a nice soft room with white sheets, oh yes."

He lay down on his bed and closed his eyes, then sat bolt upright. On the edge of hearing, he could make out a faint sound that went something like *schluppschlupp schluppschlupp.*

He shook his head wearily, thinking his ears were playing tricks on him and putting it down to the stress of the day. He gradually fell into a deep sleep, mildly tainted with nightmares of the improbably vicious punishments Draegul had in store for him if he were to sleep in tomorrow.

AZRON PUFFED the last of the cigarette and heaved himself upright again. It had been a close call with the old man, and he was almost sure he had been seen, but so far, no alarm bells had sounded. He began to make his way up the glass walls again, reflecting not for the first time that, while a glass palace might look very pretty, it was also an open invitation for a thief with the right equipment and a bit of imagination.

After what seemed like a long time, he reached the very top of Dawncastle, stained pallid silver by the light of the deadly new star. He took a moment to breathe in the thin air and enjoy the view. The distant lights of the city were far below him now, and he felt momentarily dizzy. It was like floating above a galaxy…

Taking his eyes away from the ghostly spectacle of Argustin by night, he looked down through the thick glass underneath him. It was dark below, but he continued staring until his eyes adjusted. A hint of a desk made itself apparent, and the ghostly edges of a room surrounded by bookcases. Azron grinned. It was as he had suspected

—if you were going to keep something very important in the safest place possible, you'd put it at the very top of the tallest tower. Directly beneath him was Draegul's study.

He crawled around the roof for a while, searching for a place where the glass was thinner. Sure enough, there was a skylight, the glass only a few millimeters thick.

Azron placed a suction cup on the thinner glass and took a wickedly sharp blade from his coat. The blade was pure diamond, part of a machine designed to slice through metal, and Azron had no trouble cutting a circle in the skylight big enough to slide through. He gently lifted the circle of glass free and put it by his side. Then he took the grapnel from his coat and secured it on a nearby girder. He let the rope dangle into the dark study, where it swung quietly, like a hesitant snake. Azron slid down noiselessly, a dark silhouette against the pale night sky, which was swallowed slowly and completely by the darkness of the room. He reached the floor and spread his limbs, delicately distributing his weight so that he kept low and moved silently. Immersed in blackness, he tuned his senses in to the room around him.

That was when he heard the snoring.

He stood there, rigid with the unique hybrid of fear and excitement known only to the cat burglar. He waited. Waited...

Finally, his eyes adjusted completely so that he could make out most of the room around him. He turned his head toward the sound of the snoring and detected the almost invisible sheen of black armor. There was a guard in here, something Azron had not expected. Thankfully, though, the guard wasn't very good—he was propped against the wall, having dozed off on his feet.

Azron tiptoed up to the sleeping guard, creeping so smoothly that no carpet scuff or creaking floorboard gave cause for alarm. Then, as soundlessly as ink spreading, he reached into his coat and brought out a glass phial. He covered his nose with one hand and uncorked the vial with the other. He held the vial under the guard's nose for only a second before he slumped to the floor unconscious, with a clanking of armor that might as well have been an avalanche in the nighttime quiet.

Smirking in the shadows, Azron corked the vial and returned it to the recesses of his coat. Then he turned his attention to the rest of the room. He could make out several desks and shelves, each laden with paperwork that might or might not have been important. An ordinary man might have lit a lamp and begun rummaging through them but, union or not, Azron was no ordinary man. He understood the secret to hiding valuables, and that was this: you didn't hide them in the most secure place because that was the first place a thief would look. You hid them somewhere a thief wouldn't *bother* looking. And because Azron also understood a little something about Draegul, he knew that all of the obvious strongboxes and safes were likely to contain nothing more than cunning acid traps or spring-loaded poison darts.

He scanned the room again, noting all the places you'd expect valuables to be hidden and ignoring them until, eventually, his gaze fell upon a silver tea tray. It was certainly not unfeasible that the Emperor would take tea in his study, and the sandwich crusts and biscuit crumbs gave testament to this being the case. However, Azron thought it unlikely that a man of Draegul's stature would walk into his study in the morning to find lunchtime debris from the previous day. Azron walked over to the tray and spent a good few minutes looking at things. Then he reached over to a coffee urn, opened it, and tipped it upside down.

A large rolled-up wad of papers fell onto the floor. Azron grinned like a cat and snatched them up. He couldn't make out any of the lettering in the dark and wondered if he should risk lighting a match. That was when he heard footsteps.

An ordinary thief might have frozen, waiting to see whether the steps were coming in his or her direction, but Azron was no ordinary thief. One of his greatest talents, and one he believed that no master thief could survive without, was his ability to intuitively know when to run like hell. He stuffed the papers in his coat and pulled out the Do-fer in their stead. It was already preset to the professor's laboratory, and all he had to do was punch in the activation sequence of the keypad. He keyed in the code and waited for the inevitable nausea of immediate reality transgression.

He had a brief moment of anxiety whether he had retrieved the relevant file, but dismissed it. If he had got the wrong documents—and he doubted he had—there would be no chance of returning once the break-in was discovered, so there seemed little point in worrying about it. The world began to slow around him just as the door to the study opened...

DRAEGUL UNLOCKED the door to his study with the heavy iron key that he wore around his neck at all times. It was far too late—or indeed too early—to be awake, but Draegul had been unable to sleep. The whispering in his ears had been louder and more urgent than ever. Finally, he had crawled out of bed and wandered the palace, finding himself drawn to the study.

He shivered in the chill of the upper corridors and cursed the decision to leave his chambers, where warm sheets and warmer women were readily available. Perhaps it was simply the excitement of the day that had kept him awake. Handen the adventurer had been Draegul's first real challenge in centuries, and when he had found out about his escape, the Emperor had been secretly glad. He would enjoy hunting the bastard down and having him publicly tortured.

He was confident that it would not be long before the escapees were back in his custody; the city had been put in lockdown, and the already extensive guard on the outer walls had been tripled. There was no hope of anyone leaving Argustin...at least, not in one piece.

Draegul pushed against the study door and frowned when it jammed. He pushed again, harder and harder until the heavy object slid out of the way. He hurried into the room and turned on the light. The heavy object turned out to be an unconscious guard, and by the way bubbles of spit were frothing from beneath his helmet, it was quite obvious he had been drugged.

Draegul felt the sickness of dread in his stomach, and his gaze went immediately to his tea tray. The coffee urn that had served as his hiding place was on the floor, overturned and empty. Lying by the urn on the otherwise immaculate carpet was an object that shouldn't have been there. The Emperor bent down to see it. It was a cigarette butt, still smoldering. Draegul grinned, but it was a grin with a razor edge. It was a grin that said, "Before this day is through, many, many people will die."

The whispering in his ears reached a raging crescendo.

RILEY LOOKED AT THE FILE, shuffling and sorting the papers, his brow becoming increasingly drawn with concern.

"This can't be right. You must have the wrong files!"

Azron shook his head. "Believe me, mate, I definitely had the right room, and this document was definitely never meant to fall into the wrong hands. If this isn't the paperwork you're looking for, I'll smoke my hat."

Riley shook his head again. "This is all about Operation Deadwaker. It's just a series of reports from archaeological digs in the Nastren desert."

Handen picked up one of the reports. "The pyramids?" he asked.

Riley looked through a few more of the reports. "Yes. All of them."

"Why would he be so interested in the pyramids?" said Bip.

"And why keep it such a secret?" Xharon added.

"He's looking for something," Handen murmured. "He's been digging up those pyramids for years, and according to these figures, it's costing him a pretty penny too…"

"Never met a penny that wasn't pretty," said Azron, smiling.

"What could be so important to him that he'd spend so much time and money exhuming ancient tombs?"

"Treasure?" suggested Xharon. "Or curiosity, maybe?"

"Or perhaps an ancient weapon left here eons ago by beings from another world?" offered Bip.

The doomsayers paused, each silent as they contemplated what had just been said.

"Just a guess," added Bip.

"Of course!" said Handen. "Maybe the Discordance weren't corrupting Draegul to *build* a weapon, just to *use* one! One that has already been built for them!"

Riley arched his eyebrows. "It would make more sense," he said. "I'm not entirely sure if even the finest scientific minds in Bersch could build a weapon that could safely destroy an astral disaster of this magnitude—by all that's precarious, I couldn't be *certain*. Far safer to have an ace in the hand, as it were, than to gamble blindly."

"Or, as my dad used to say, better to knock someone unconscious than to rely on them being asleep," said Azron.

"Erm…yes. That works, too, I suppose…"

"Let me get this straight," Xharon interjected. "These Discordance chaps are a race of super-beings who want to see the universe descend into absolute chaos and general disharmony, so part of their plan is to influence my uncle, over the course of a thousand years, so that he could eventually discover a weapon that would not only allow him to save his planet from oblivion, but also to destroy the very stars in the sky and inadvertently cause a pointless interstellar war that could kill trillions?"

"Yes?"

"Right. Right. Just making sure I was up to speed. Carry on."

"Okay…"

"Wait a minute!"

"Yes, Xharon?"

"Why don't they just do it themselves?"

Handen sighed. "They exist on a different material plane to our universe—they can't physically affect anything here."

"Then how are they controlling Uncle Tommy?"

"They're not controlling him. They've merely used constant subliminal mental influence to ensure he became an all-powerful megalomaniac with no conscience and a penchant for destroying things."

"So…strictly speaking, this isn't really Uncle Tommy's fault, yes?"

Handen rolled his eyes. "If I told you to shoot a man, it'd be *you* who pulled the trigger, not me. The Discordance can influence things, yes, but they can't turn a decent man into a cold-blooded mass-murderer any more than they could convince a rock to turn into a beaver. We are all accountable for our actions, regardless of influence."

"Oh…" said Xharon. She looked downcast.

Bip put a hand on her shoulder. "Think of it this way; if weakness were the rotten wood in an otherwise fine piece of timber, then the Discordance are the termites that are drawn to that weakness, sooner or later destroying the whole piece of wood."

Xharon frowned. "So you're saying Uncle Tommy's got termites?"

Bip thought for a minute. "Yes. In a manner of speaking."

Azron coughed in the puzzled silence. "I think we've gone a bit off-topic here, chaps. We were talking about the end of the world, yeah?"

"See here!" cried Riley, holding up a sheet of paper from the Dead-waker file. "I think I've found something!"

The others crowded around while Ridley smoothed the paper over his desk.

"Look at this report. Highly unusual, by all accounts, and from the Grand Tutor himself."

Bip read the last report aloud. "A tomb of unprecedented size and unusual material…of unknown origin and estimated to be older than recorded civilization…investigations continue…await further reports."

"Looks as though this is our tomb," said Handen.

"How can we be sure?" said Riley. "What if this is really just one of Draegul's bizarre and expensive hobbies, merely an enthusiastic interest in archaeology? Doesn't anyone else feel we're being awfully presumptuous, here?"

Handen tapped a finger on another section of report, which depicted a few rows of unusual symbols. "Here," he said.

The professor squinted at the lettering, adjusting the lenses on his tentacle-framed glasses. "It is a sample of some hieroglyphics," he said. "I'm afraid I'm not familiar with them."

Handen smiled. "They're hieroglyphics of a sort, but not the kind you'd find on this world…"

"What do you mean?"

"It's a very old form of Standard."

"Standard?"

"Yes. An intergalactic language unification code, designed to be a common ground of communication across hundreds of civilizations."

Riley's eyes shone with awe. "An alien language. Can you decipher it?"

"Not with complete accuracy—it's very old…" explained Handen.

"What do you think it says?"

"Like I said, it's a rough translation, but at a guess, I'd say it seems to be a warning."

"What kind of warning?"

Handen looked down at the writing, eyes narrowed in concentration. "Danger: Aim Away From Face."

The doomsayers looked at one another.

"Well," Azron said eventually, "I think that about clears it up."

Bip grinned. "We've found our weapon."

IN THE SILENT folds of dimensional infinity, Mr. Random fumed. He fumed neither quietly nor privately. Part of the charm of living in a different plane of existence is that you can scream as loudly and for as long as you like.

He had been so close, *so close* to destroying the last of the resistance to his plans! It was distressing, it was annoying, it was infuriating, and most of all… it was *insulting*. Yes, insulting. Bip Plunkerton's stubborn refusal to die in the face of innumerable instances of likely doom was mockingly *random*. His sheer defiance of the odds was totally against the order of causality. In a normal, sane, and well-ordered world, Bip would be *dead, dead, dead!* And yet here he was, completely and ridiculously alive!

That was the problem with an ordered universe that ran on specific rules—just when you thought you had it pinned down, it went and did something completely unexpected. That was why you had to rout for the random, that was why you trusted in uncertainty—because order was a *lie*.

The truth was chaos, pure and simple, but the world could be tricky that way. It was like one of those toy pictures that seemed to be a haphazard static of color, but if you let your eyes relax, suddenly there was a 3-D picture of a donkey or something. Mr. Random had always thoroughly despised such pictures. Why degrade the purity of static with a donkey?

Things were meant to be stupid and unexpected and generally badly run—he *knew* tha, knew it in the core of his being. It was his job...no, it was his *duty* to make sure that the ultraverse understood that as well, and stopped—for just one buggering minute—pretending otherwise. And yet this young boy and his *stupid* friends were still alive despite innumerable odds that should, if the world would play by its own rules for just one second, have killed them a thousand times over. The whole affair seemed to suggest that there was some greater cosmic goal or narrative toward which they worked toward, and frankly, Mr. Random found that idea unforgivably offensive.

You can't pretend it is fate; it is luck. There is no quest, only a series of loosely connected events. There can be no story; the universe is not as simple as that.

At least, it shouldn't be...

Mr. Random took a deep breath and watched his shaking hand. His head was beginning to hurt.

"*Tup tup a looba doo,*" he sang. "*Tup tup a looba doo, violently blue, and rabbits too, because that's what we shoe, shoe, great big shoe.*"

He felt a little better. The song didn't make any sense, and that was why he liked it. He knew that, secretly, no words made sense, that symbol and reaction were processes unique to an individual, that meaning was merely a pretentious perception, a case of developed semantics. There was no meaning. *Tup tup a loo, no meaning for you.*

He raised a hand to his head again, but the headache was fading. The nonsense ditty had calmed him somewhat. Now he could concentrate. The plan was nearly complete, and it didn't matter if there were people who thought they could stop it. Mr. Random had all the pieces, and he didn't play by the rules. Draegul would find the weapon, as had been decreed a thousand years ago, then Bersch would fulfill its destiny as a bringer of chaos.

Still, it would be better to see Bip's cold, dead eyes. Just to be safe and sure. Just to relax a little. Better to stare into his frightened, dying eyes and be sure of uncertainty.

Tup tup a loo.

HANDEN SLID the prototype pistolas into the twin holsters at his hips and placed his blade in the scabbard across his back. He had changed back into his leathers, worn hard and rugged by travel and battle. He coiled the bullwhip at his side and touched the hilts of the various daggers and knives concealed about his person. Draegul would come for them soon, and he would come fast and merciless. Handen was prepared.

Azron readied himself too, checking the grappling hook in the folds of his coat, his various vials, picks and tools, and finally his dagger. It was a dagger that was new and unscathed, gleaming and smooth. This was because it was a dagger that had never been used. Azron was a thief—that was all he had ever wanted to be, and he knew how easy it was for some thieves to cross the line between mugging and grievous bodily harm. Those were thieves with no class, union allocated or otherwise. He sighed as he checked the still-sharp edge of the dagger, a weapon bought long ago "just in case." And now it seemed that "just in case" might be just around the corner. Azron wondered whether he were the kind of thief who could steal a life...

Xharon, wearing an outfit that could only serve as a distraction, whirled her axes around her in a hurricane of cutting edges. The kata always made her feel confident. Here, fending off and countering imaginary attacks, she was unbeatable. All too soon, it seemed, she would find out just how unbeatable she was.

Bip had prepared himself too, though the only weapon he wore was Brian, the familiar blade that was still, thankfully, unsullied by combat. He slipped his rucksack onto his back, not realizing how naked he had felt without it. He didn't have much to carry these days. At the end of his journey, he bore none of his original provisions. Gone were the corned-beef sandwiches, re-programmed acorns, and his heavy furs. Gone too was the Infamous Goose; lost to celebration, boredom, and yetis. Gone was his hat, which he missed and regretted exploding. There was little left of the possessions of the boy who had set off from Kaneq what seemed a lifetime ago. Other than his sword, only his spectacles and his rucksack remained. In the prelude to what seemed to be the final leg of his journey, he drew comfort from these items. He rested his hands easily on the pommel of Brian and, though he knew he would probably never use the blade for the purpose Rynford had intended it, he found comfort there too.

Riley fiddled with the Do-fer, readjusting his multi-faceted spectacles while he tried to estimate the trans-dimensional co-ordinates for the location of the pyramid. He didn't have much to work with, since the pyramids were miles away and the only dimensional references he had were very local, but he believed he was making progress. The occasional and positive *blint* and *whirr* from the Do-fer was an encouraging sign.

Eventually the professor looked up from his tinkering. "I believe I have a rough estimate," he said.

"How rough?" asked Handen.

Riley scratched at his brow. "There are so many factors to consider..." he began. "Real space in relation to phase space, estimating frequencies and bandwidths..."

"*How rough?*"

"We could materialize anywhere within a few miles of the pyramid, by all that's inconvenient."

Handen nodded. "All the more reason to get going as soon as possible. Now, is everyone ready?"

The doomsayers nodded in unison. Handen looked at them, his friends and colleagues. It was not the first time he had led them into danger, and he knew that, once again, they would follow. But he had to give them a chance anyway. "Look, by now Draegul knows we have the paperwork; therefore, he knows that we know the whereabouts of the weapon. Chances are he's on his way to the pyramid, most likely with a small army in tow. We have the advantage of the Do-fer, but I can't be sure how long it will be before they catch us up…"

Xharon cocked her head slightly. "Is there something you want to say?" she said, challenging him.

Handen shook his head. "I just want you to be ready for anything. It's all down to us now, and we have to be prepared."

"You mean expect the unexpected?" said Bip.

"I suppose so, yes," Handen conceded.

Azron sighed. "Never liked that phrase," he muttered. "I mean, what if I expect to transform into a cloud of fish-shaped bubbles and float off to the moon? I mean it's just not likely is it? So what's the point of wasting imagination expecting something that's clearly not going to happen?"

There was a long pause, broken by a discreet cough from Xharon. "That was an unusually pointless and pedantic statement, Azron, even for you."

The thief sighed. "I know. It's just this whole 'bravely facing certain death' thing. It's got me out of sorts, you know."

"I would have thought you would have been used to the idea by now…"

Azron shrugged. "I suppose I'm just stuck in my ways."

"Well," said Bip, "with any luck, this will be the last time we risk our lives for the greater good."

"That's what I'm afraid of…" Azron mumbled.

The conversation was suddenly cut off by a familiar low hum.

"The Do-fer is ready," cried Professor Riley. "Prepare yourselves."

"You're absolutely sure this will get us to the pyramids?" asked Bip.

"The odds are very nearly almost likely," said Riley.

"Oh...good?"

"Remember," said Handen. "It's hot where we're going, so be prepared for the sudden climate change."

Bip nodded absent-mindedly, concentrating on the growing whistle of the Do-fer and preparing himself for the unpleasantness of immediate reality transgression lag. He just had time to register that something didn't quite feel right when the world slowed down around him...

Before him, as tiny black lines began to etch their way across his vision, he caught a brief glimpse of a metal smirk.

MR. RANDOM WATCHED in fascination as the Do-fer began to work. Unlike the people of Bersch, Random didn't need special equipment to see and surf the dimensional folds, but it was interesting to see how the machine suddenly bent the universe around itself, propelling its operators into the insulating ether around the realities. The device was a clear advantage that would see the doomsayers arrive in the desert a day or so ahead of Draegul's forces. That was, if the device worked *correctly*...

Focusing on the bending lines of reality around him, Mr. Random reached out and plucked a few like the strings of a brilliant and alien harp. Ironically, what he was about to do was a feat that would have been beyond his powers if not for the aid of the professor's machine. Random, as with all of the Discordance, had only limited influence in Bersch's dimensional plane, but now, strictly speaking, Bip and his companions were no longer in that dimension—they were a hair's breadth outside it, and that made all the difference.

The Discordant chuckled to himself as he plucked haphazardly at the visible frequencies around him, the quantum strings of reality. He had no idea where the doomsayers would end up, but it would be a time and place far away from the pyramids of Nastre.

7

Destiny and Self-Perpetuating Time Loops

Before he had even had a chance to recover from the disorientation and nausea, the cold hit him like a punch in the stomach. He doubled over, wrapping his arms around himself and shivering. He peered around desperately while trying in vain to shield his face from the stinging wind. The world was white around him, and for a terrifying moment, Bip was sure he had gone blind. He jerked around as a hand grabbed his shoulder and came face to face with Azron, who bore the expression of complete and utter seriousness worn by those who are unreasonably cold.

"This is not the bloody desert!" shouted the thief, barely controlling the chattering of his teeth. "I realize that's stating the obvious, but I thought it was worth pointing out. In fact, it's worth saying again; *this is not the bloody desert*! In fact, it's the complete bloody opposite!"

Before he could reply, Bip felt another hand on his shoulder. He turned to see Handen and Riley emerge from the snowstorm.

"Technically, that's bot true!" Shouted Riley. "You see, a desert doesn't necessarily–"

"There's been a mistake!" Handen interrupted. "Wherever this is, I think it's safe to say it's not where we wanted to go."

Bip nodded dumbly. "Yes, Azron was just saying…"

Riley looked down at the machine. "This makes no sense. By all that's preposterous, *this makes no sense!* How could my calculations have been so drastically askew?"

Bip had a recollection of the sudden sheen of a metal grin. "Random," he muttered.

"What?" cried Azron.

"Nothing, it doesn't matter now. Where's Xharon?"

"H-h-h-h…" came a voice from behind them.

They turned to see Xharon, eyes wide with shock, clinging desperately to an over-exposed body that was rapidly turning blue.

"H-he-heh…here!"

Handen quickly removed his outer coat and wrapped it around the girl's shoulders.

"You see?" said Riley. "This is why you shouldn't wander around in your knickers!"

"What are we going to do?" said Azron.

"Huddle together," said Handen. "We need to share our body heat."

The group huddled together like the characters of a feel-good sitcom, collective teeth chattering manically as the snow whipped around them.

"W-w-w…where are we?" managed Xharon.

"The Ice Plains! It has to be!" wailed Bip. "I'm right back where I started from!"

Handen leaned down toward Riley, who was still fiddling with the Do-fer.

"Professor, how long 'til you can get us back?"

Riley shook his head. "The device was never meant to operate in such conditions—the mechanisms are extremely delicate!"

"What are you saying?"

Riley looked at Handen with despair in his eyes. "It's frozen up!"

Handen tried to grit his teeth in frustration but succeeded only in chattering them more rapidly.

"We need to get warm, fast, otherwise we won't last a minute out here."

"I don't suppose anyone thought to bring a coal-heater or something?" asked Azron.

"No."

"Then how? How do we make heat?"

As one, the group turned their heads slowly to Bip.

"What?" he said nervously.

"Oh come on, mate!" said Azron. "If there's one thing you're good at, it's making fire."

"There's a chance I might blow us all to pieces!" Bip protested.

"At least we'll die warm!"

"Okay, okay!" said Bip, thinking desperately. "I'll need a fuel source or something. It's one thing to create fire, but another to sustain it."

"I'll ask again," said Azron. "Did anyone think to bring some coal or suchlike?"

Handen ignored his companion's sarcastic jibes and scanned the snowy tundra around them. It was difficult to see anything through the swirling snow, but he thought he could make out a dark bump in the ground several dozen feet away.

"Come on!" he shouted, and led the group, shuffling forward like some drunken, multi-limbed beast.

As they approached the dark hunk in the snow, it became abundantly clear that they had indeed traveled back to the Ice Plains—before them lay the hulking corpse of a driftdigger, its buck teeth pointing skyward. Bip blanched at a sudden stench and realized that the creature's belly had been torn open and partially eaten. The steam rising from the wounds indicated that it was a fairly fresh kill, but there were more pressing concerns than possible lurking predators.

Bip thought back to his training with Rynford. "The coat!" he said. "Its coat contains a natural fuel—if we can ignite that, it'll burn for hours!"

"D-d-d..." began Xharon.

"Do it!" finished Azron.

Bip approached the corpse and tried his best to focus his mind. It was difficult to ignore the frantic shaking of his muscles, but he managed to make contact with the physical essence of the corpse.

There was still warmth in the beast, faint but shining, like a beacon in the deathly cold around it. He closed his eyes and concentrated.

Concentrated...

He felt the impact of the explosion before he heard the noise and was thrown onto his back. He looked up into a roaring bonfire that smelled of cooked meat and Kaneqian lamp oil.

"Yes!" he shouted, pumping his fist in the air. "I did it!"

The doomsayers stood around the burning body, relishing the comforting heat.

"Now that's *better*," said Azron, rubbing his hands together. "Well done, mate," he added.

"Professor?" said Handen.

Riley waved his hand, not looking up from the Do-fer. "Fifteen minutes or so. I still need to reset the frequency parameters."

Handen nodded and looked around. He turned to Bip. "Funny we should end up back here, don't you think?"

Bip didn't answer. Now that he wasn't freezing to death, he was taking the time to look around the tundra. "We should be near Kaneq," he said. "I'm sure of it."

Handen looked around. Being back on the Ice Plains was coaxing out long-dormant memories, but they were still hazy. "Are you certain?" he said.

Bip nodded and pointed toward a mountain. "That's Old Bachalack," he said, then swung his arm around to the east, pointing to another mountain. "And that's the Patient Mother. And look—we're quite close to the cliff-face and the frozen lake. Kaneq should be somewhere very near."

"How can you tell?" said Xharon, moving closer to the conversation.

Bip shrugged. "I was raised here," he said. "Every morning I woke up to the same two mountains looking over me."

Handen scanned the open plain, squinting with effort. "I don't see anything," he said. "Maybe you're mistaken."

Bip shook his head, his expression becoming increasingly troubled. "It's not as if you can just misplace an entire village," he said.

"There were dozens of houses, and larger buildings too, like the Dome. Not to mention the heatshield. If we are where I think we are, Kaneq should be very close. In fact, we're practically right on top of it."

"Maybe they left. You have been away for a while," offered Xharon.

"If they left, I doubt they would have taken their houses with them," said Bip. "That's not something you can just put in your rucksack, really."

Handen put a hand on his friend's shoulder. "If they left, they would have disengaged the heatshield. How long do you think it would have taken for the houses to be buried under the snow?"

Bip stared for a long while at the surrounding expanse of snow and ice. This was his home, which he had ventured into dangerous lands to save. To think that it had been abandoned and left to the slow and constant ravages of the Ice Plains was unbearable.

"No," he said. "No!"

Bip ran out into the blizzard and began digging frantically in the snow.

"No, no, *no!*"

Handen ran after him, lifting him from the cold ground as he struggled. "Listen to me, Bip—listen! I could be wrong—we could be wrong!"

Bip struggled out of the bigger man's grip and sat down in the snow, defeated, tears forming in his eyes. "No," he whispered. "This is where I left my home. This is where I left my family, my friends...*everything!*" He put his head in his hands. "I was supposed to save them—I was supposed to come back a hero! And now it's all gone. It's all gone..."

Handen took the weeping Kaneqian by arm and led him slowly back toward the fire. "If there's an explanation, we'll find it," he said. "If your friends are alive out there, we'll find them. I promise."

Bip said nothing, only stared into the bonfire that was even now beginning to dwindle.

There was a rumble from the skies. Something distant and powerful.

Azron looked up. "That's all we need, a bloody storm."

The thunder roll continued, rising in volume, and the ground beneath them began to shake.

"That's no storm," Handen breathed.

The doomsayers turned toward the sound, a rumble like a stampede of giants from somewhere behind the mass of the Patient Mother. There was a bright flash from behind the mountain and a short burst of noise that peaked temporarily over the constant rumbling.

Some long-dead association triggered deep in Handen's psyche.

"Kanick..."

And then it came. A giant, silvery, elongated disc, still glowing and smoking from its dramatic tussle with the atmosphere, narrowly avoiding the tip of the mountain as it swooped toward the tundra in a blaze of gravity.

Riley gaped. "Astonishing," he said. "By all that is astonishing, this is far and away—*the most astonishing thing I have ever seen.*"

"What is it?" cried Bip.

Handen grabbed the younger man by the shoulder. "It's the *Sentinel!*" he yelled. "Your family haven't left—they haven't even been born yet!"

Confusion quickly blanketed Bip's face.

"Don't you see?" yelled Handen. "All of this has already happened! This is when the *Sentinel* crashed a thousand years ago! We've traveled back in time! A thousand years back in time!"

THE *SENTINEL* SCREAMED toward the ground, its repellent fields directed entirely over its underbelly and nose. Inside, Finnegun checked their velocity one last time and quickly worked out the probability of surviving such a crash. *It would be fifty per cent,* he thought, *if we weren't heading toward a cliff face and consequently a thousand-foot drop onto a massive lake of ice.*

With an unfathomable boom, the craft plunged into the snowy

ground, its shielding causing gigantic clods of earth to be ploughed up in front of it. The momentum of the impact sent the vessel crashing through ice and snow toward the sheer cliff face at an alarming rate.

"THEY'RE NOT GOING to make it!" shouted Bip. "They'll fly right over the edge!"

"Do something!" cried Xharon.

Handen held a hand to his head. Memories were coming back to him in a confused tumble. "They must make it! We survived the crash; otherwise, I wouldn't be here!"

Bip wasn't listening; his mind was entirely focused on the problem of stopping a gigantic spaceship from sliding to an icy grave. He reached out with his mind, searching for something, anything he could use. All he found was snow.

The words of his psyence tutor Glimton came back to him in a sudden vivid display.

"Your problem, you talentless idiot, is that you're so busy concentrating on concentrating *that you completely miss what it is you're supposed to be doing!"*

The words hadn't made sense to him then—just another of Glimton's lunatic monologues—but now, now something inside him seemed to reveal itself, something that had always been there but he had never acknowledged.

He didn't need to concentrate.

He completely didn't *concentrate…*

WITHIN THE FOREDECK, Finnegun closed his eyes once again. There was no way, he thought, that they could possibly slow down in time to avoid sliding over the cliff. As a sense of finality washed over him, Finnegun opened one of his eyes, determined, at least, to face his fate head-on. He was surprised to see that the landscape had changed slightly—where before there had been an empty expanse between the tobogganing ship and the cliff, there was now a gigantic, oddly-shaped snowdrift...

THE GROUND SHOOK, and Bip gasped as the air was suddenly sucked from his lungs. Near the edge of the cliff, the air shimmered and fogged and seemed to solidify.

"Great holy bastards," breathed Azron. "What on Bersch is that?"

Riley stood transfixed. "It's an igloo, by all that's preposterously unexpected! *It's the biggest igloo in existence!*"

FINNEGUN HAD JUST enough time to wonder where it had come from before the *Sentinel*, smashing clouds of ice into the air, collided with the mysterious snowdrift with an odd suddenness and a sound that can only be described as a colossal...

THERE IS a race of beings in the ultraverse known as the Documenters. It is the lot of this ancient, immortal, and near-omniscient species to catalog the comings and goings of existence in a library that is so huge it has a dimension all to itself. A particular faction of the Documenters were watching the events on the Ice Plains with great interest—they were the Order of the Onomatopoeic, whose responsibility it was to give a name to every sound ever made. Even so, with uncountable years of experience, and talents far beyond the reach of most life forms, they found it difficult to come up with a suitable onomatopoeia for a massive, red-hot spaceship suddenly colliding with a likewise massive freshly materialized igloo.

The best they could come up with was "*rrrRRrCraushtinkly-winklyPOFF!!*"

It was a decision the merits of which would be argued long into eternity.

BIP SANK TO HIS KNEES, his head swimming from the curious disassociation he felt with the world before him. There, exactly where he had left it, was the Dome. True, it was larger and rougher than the giant snow-mound he would come to know so many years from now, but it was unmistakably Kaneq's landmark building. He wondered whether anyone would believe him, if he ever made it back to his own time…

He was suddenly hauled up by his arms. Handen looked into his eyes with an expression of fierce concentration.

"No time to lie down, kid. It's not over yet."

Bip shook the mugginess from his head. "What now?" he said.

"It's come back to me," said Handen excitedly. "It's all come back to me. They're trapped under tons of snow in there, and you've got to help them out."

"Me? Why me?"

"Because that's the way it happened. I don't think I should say any more, but you've got to go and talk to those people."

"Can't you come with me?"

Handen laughed. "Of course not, reason being that *I'm already in there!*"

Bip looked around helplessly. "Well, what do I do?"

"I honestly don't know," said Handen. "All I know is that you do it."

Bip glanced from his friend's face to the pile of snow that would one day be the epicenter of his home. He turned back to his friends, who looked at him with something new in their faces, something that had not been there before. It was awe.

"I'll just be off then, shall I?" said Bip.

His companions nodded slowly. "Good luck," said Xharon.

Bip tramped off into the snow, the firelight lashing softly at his retreating back. He paused as he heard the cramping footsteps of someone jogging up behind him and turned to see Handen approach.

The brief joviality had left the older man's face. "One more thing. I need you to promise me something."

"Yes?"

"When you see me in there, don't say anything. Don't let me know who you are. Don't mention your name, don't let me know about… me. Promise me that."

Bip shrugged. "That is a really confusing request, when you think about it."

"Don't think about it. Just promise."

Bip looked into the unwavering gaze of his companion. "Sure, Handen."

The bigger man nodded and turned back toward the fire. Bip turned back toward the dark.

DARKNESS.

A nagging sensation that he had something to be getting on with.

More darkness.

An awareness of cold. A problem in the chronostatic chamber. Not supposed to feel. Pain. Pain in his leg and neck.

Darkness.

"Captain?"

BIP APPROACHED THE DOME, sensing the faint signatures of heat coming from the crashed ship beneath its icy blanket. He didn't feel the cold, and perhaps wouldn't be surprised to know that a firedance tumbled slowly about his shoulders, responding to his unconscious will. Bip wasn't entirely sure how he had accessed so much of his latent knack and wasn't sure if he'd be able to do it again, but for now, the residual energies of his psyentific feat seemed to be responding to his thoughts almost without him realizing it.

He waved a hand at the surface of the snow dome and, quickly and without fanfare, a staircase began to form on the icy walls. He walked up them, careful not to think too hard about what he was doing. It was, he thought, like balancing a ball on his head—if he thought too hard about the ball, it would surely drop.

He reached the top of the mound that would one day become the Dome and was faintly surprised to see a flock of penguins, seemingly totally bewildered by their current predicament. They were not the fat and fluffy domesticated penguins of a future Kaneq, but their sleek and oily ancestors. One of them quacked indignantly at him.

Ignoring the stranded birds, Bip walked to the center of the Dome and stood for a while, gazing downward. Then, taking care not to concentrate, he made a shovel shape with his hands and a digging motion through the air before him. Responding to an unexpected reconstruction of the air molecules around it, the snow atop the downed spacecraft was scooped up and dispersed into the winds, leaving a deep crater. Bip repeated the motion, digging with re-directed molecular energy, cutting into the snow rhythmically and methodically until he stood on the cusp of a large inverted cone.

The penguins, finally succumbing to dumb curiosity, came to stare at the newcomer and the large cave he had fashioned, gaggling and sliding around with all the grace of a creature that, though born to ice, still had a love/hate relationship with it. Unsurprisingly, many slipped down into Bip's hole, quacking madly and landing with soft thuds. Bip watched as the snow around them began to shift like quicksand, then followed them down.

THERE WAS AN ODD THUMPING SOUND, like the shuffling of gigantic feet. The crew fell silent, listening carefully as the noise grew louder. After quite some time, a flurry of snow began to cascade into the ship from the access hatch until a hollow was made near the exit. A weak light and a bitter wind swept into the foredeck.

Completely against everyone's expectations, a penguin plummeted from the sky and landed with a bang on the ship's deck, followed by several others, which proceeded to wallow around in confusion, quacking with the attitude of animals that have nothing better to do than quack. Finnegun tried to think when he had last seen penguins…

After a few minutes and several more confused penguins, a face dangled from the top of the hatch—a face that Finnegun found disturbingly familiar.

"All right?" said Bip.

The crew of the *Sentinel* turned to Finnegun. The captain seemed to cogitate on the problem.

"Yes," he concluded.

"Good, good," said Bip. "That's good, then."

"And may I ask who you are?" asked Finnegun.

"Who, me?" Bip thought for a moment. "My name is not important."

"That's an unusual name," said Izzy, irritation still heavy in her voice.

Bip stared for a while, surprised by his calmness. *These are the founders*, he thought. *These are my ancestors, and I've just saved their lives! How weird is that?*

He took in the boiler-suit-style uniforms of the crew and found them strangely disappointing. Even after he had learned that the founders were from another world, he had still envisioned them as rugged pioneers, packs laden for long travel and faces harsh from foreign winds. The clean-cut and soberly uniformed collection of space-farers before him were a far cry from the mighty gypsies of his mind.

Except for one. One bore the expression of things seen and done. One bore the stare of those who look for danger and know where to find it. Bip's world went fuzzy as Handen Strike stepped forward. He looked different—perhaps five or so years younger, his features less travel-worn and his hair shorter—but the poise and stare of the soon-to-be immortal was unmistakable.

Bip swallowed. Before him was a man who had no idea what the world had in store for him, the sacrifices he would make and the horrors he would face. The burden of lifetimes. How could this man forgive him, for knowing what dangers awaited him and saying nothing? But, of course, had already forgiven him. And made him promise…

Bip realized he had been staring at Handen. The man frowned under the scrutiny and approached Finnegun's side, leaning in to speak quietly in his ear.

"Sir?"

Finnegun was visibly shaken from his own contemplation. "Yes, Mr. Strike?"

"I think it would be a good idea to scout around up top, sir, see what we're up against."

Finnegun nodded. "Very well. All those who are able to, salvage what you can from the analysis equipment, don an environment suit, and prepare to touch new ground." Around him, the crew scattered in various directions until there was nobody in the room but Handen, Finnegun, Bip, and a few befuddled penguins. The penguins quacked in the manner of creatures that might quite happily quack for all eternity.

The captain turned to Bip, who was still hanging from the top of the doorway.

"You may come in if you want," he said.

"No, it's okay," said Bip. "I don't think I'll be staying long."

"Then I suppose I must thank you now," said Finnegun.

"Sorry?" said Bip. He was beginning to feel uncomfortable under Handen's cold stare. It is a uniquely disturbing feeling when a close friend looks at you like a stranger.

"For aiding us. For digging us out," Finnegun continued. "We must thank you and your people for your help."

"Oh, I don't really have any people at the moment," said Bip. "I'm just sort of passing through with a few friends."

Handen raised an eyebrow. "Passing through?"

"Yes."

"Hundreds of miles of desolate wasteland, and you're just passing through?"

"Yep."

Thankfully, at that moment, the crew began to return, each holding a different piece of sensory equipment and a floppy, rubber-like affair that served as an environment suit.

"Perhaps we'll continue this discussion up-top," said Finnegun.

THE CREW of the *Sentinel* stood on top of their fallen ship and surveyed the Ice Plains. The storm had died down now, and the frozen expanse before them twinkled in the fresh starlight like something beautifully asleep. Finnegun was propped against a crutch, taking reports, and noting down information on a wrist-console.

The temporary base at the top of the dome was lit and warmed by gel-heaters, even though the environment suits were sufficient to keep the cold at bay. The crew attended various gadgets.

The younger Handen looked up from a small palm-held device. "I'm reading limited lifeforms to the east and west, Captain. Small groups here and there, larger than a usual animal pack but smaller than a nomadic tribe..."

"That'd be the yetis," Bip said matter-of-factly.

"Yetis?" asked Handen.

"Yeah, they're great big hairy things with bad tempers and big appetites. I'd leave them well alone, if I were you. We call them yetis."

Do we? thought Bip. *Do we call them yetis? I only call them yetis because that's what my elders called them—but what if I'd decided to tell this captain that they were called shockpigs? Or budgies? Would the me of the future still call them yetis?*

Bip shook his head. He was learning quickly that time travel was a messy business and thought that the less time he spent with these people, the better.

"Look, I've got to go," he said.

"Go?" said Finnegun. "Go where?"

Bip pointed to the distant bonfire where his friends were still waiting. "My friends and I, we have...a boat. But it's only big enough for the few of us. We're heading south. There are other lands there."

Finnegun nodded. "And what is it that you are not telling me, my strange new friend?"

Bip looked at the ground. He felt an odd reluctance to lie to this stranger, this man whose eyes he had once seen through on an ancient computer, this founder of everything he knew.

"I can't tell you much. I can only say that there aren't any people around here and that..." Bip looked at the crew, busying themselves with analysis and sensor-readings. Did he have the heart to tell them they were to die here, in the cold, never to see their homes again? No. No he did not. "I wouldn't expect to leave any time soon."

"And what's that supposed to mean?" Handen growled, suddenly annoyed. "How do you know so much about it?"

"I can't say, really. I'm sorry, but I have to go now." Bip turned and walked the steps he had fashioned earlier. Handen and Finnegun watched him leave.

"Do you want me to get him back?" said Handen.

Finnegun looked down at his feet. A penguin was shuffling idly across his boots. "No," he said. "He rescued us, after all, and I don't think we have the right to harangue him."

Handen nodded a reluctant agreement.

"Besides," continued Finnegun, smirking, "don't you think he looked rather familiar?"

"Yes," said Handen. "He looked a lot like you."

Finnegun chuckled. "I like a good mystery," he said. "And I've a feeling that this conundrum will unravel itself in the fullness of time. Have patience, Mr. Strike—it will all come clear in the end."

"DID YOU SEE THEM?" asked Xharon excitedly. "Did you see the founders? Your ancestors?"

Bip nodded.

Azron puffed on a cigarette he'd managed to light with an ember of dead driftdigger. "Well, spare us the suspense, mate—what were they like?"

Bip thought for a while. "Quite pleasant, actually. Seemed like a nice bunch."

"Did you see Handen?" said Xharon.

"Yes, he was very…like Handen, you know."

"This is incredible—*incredible!*" said Riley. "Actual time travel! This is challenging stuff, you know—*challenging stuff!* I'd always assumed that space and time were completely interrelated, but here we are, traveling through the same physical dimension but in a different time! This will require extensive study—months and months of *extensive study!*"

"I'll remind you, Professor, that if we don't get back soon, we may not have months and months of time left," Handen interrupted. "The reason being that there's still a giant nuclear asteroid to take care of."

"Of course, of course, *of course*—how silly of me. Just give me a moment, and I'll have us back in the right time in two shakes of the tail of some sort of infantile woolly quadruped."

Azron spoke. "What I don't understand is, if we're back in time, and that lot want to save the world, same as we do, why don't we just go and tell them about Draegul and everything? I mean, we could save you a lot of bother, couldn't we, Handen? We could just tell the other you where the fountain of death is and get him to invite Draegul around for a tea-party, sort of thing."

"That's a good point," Xharon agreed.

Handen shook his head. "You'd be interfering with more probability lines, repercussive ripples, and consequence cycles than you could possibly imagine."

"Oh yeah?" said Azron. "And how come you're an expert on time travel all of a sudden?"

"Oh, I'm no expert, but everyone takes at least a basic tutorial in time travel theory at the academy. It's routine."

"Really?"

"Yes, you never know when you'll be sucked through a wormhole and inadvertently find yourself at the dawn of creation."

"Happen a lot, does it?"

"Once or twice. The important thing to remember is that if you make significant changes to a society in the past, then the future results will always be impossible to predict, so it's best to leave well enough alone."

Xharon opened her mouth to protest.

"He's right, of course," said Riley. "If Draegul had been eliminated at such an early stage, then you and I, Xharon, would be very different people, I would never have been a duke, you never a princess. Perhaps never born. The same goes for Bip—if the founders had achieved their goal so early in their stay, they might never have seen the necessity for settling here, and Bip's Kaneq would never have existed. And then who's to say that, with Draegul destroyed, another ruler would not have risen in his place and attracted the attention of the Discordance? The possibilities are endless, and there is no way we could guarantee a successful future, no matter how carefully we planned it."

Azron blew out his cheeks in exasperation. "Well, bang goes that argument, then," he said.

"Well, no, hang on..." began Xharon. "If that's the case, then Bip saving his ancestors must have already have happened if we're to live in the future we know, and if it already happened, then what's just happened now?"

Riley put a reassuring arm around his daughter's shoulders. "It raises all sorts of questions, yes. The very fact that Bip saved his ancestors means that he was always destined to save his ancestors. Think of it as fate, if it suits you better."

"Like destiny?"

"Yes," said Riley. "Though you could also call it a self-perpetuating time-loop, if you wanted to be more accurate."

There was a silence.

"I think I'll stick to destiny," said Xharon.

Handen turned to Bip as if suddenly remembering something. "Did you see Finnegun?"

Bip nodded. "Yes, he looked familiar, somehow..."

Handen grinned widely. "That's because he looked just like you!"

"Really?"

"It came back to me, the reason you looked so familiar the first time I saw you. You must be directly descended from him."

"You really think so?"

"Yes, it's likely—the resemblance is very strong."

"What was he like?" asked Bip.

Handen smiled fondly. "He was a brilliant man, and I'm sure he'd be proud to call you his descendant."

There was a silence, warm despite the surrounding cold.

Riley coughed politely. "The device is ready, reset to our original intended co-ordinates. We can leave at any time."

Xharon hugged the penguin closer to her. "Good," she said. "It's bally well freezing again."

Handen clapped his hands together. "Then let's go. We've a dramatic rescue to initiate. One a thousand years in the making." He turned to look at Bip, a glint in his eye that hinted at pride. "And not the first one today, either."

The Do-fer began to hum, and soon the world wavered around them. And then they were gone.

8

Back to the Bone Desert

Draegul stood at the head of the dirigible *Fierce Reprisal*, the wind flickering his long, raven hair as the city of Argustin peaked and troughed below him with metropolitan symmetry. Behind him, the airboat armada of Argustin—the fastest, fiercest, and most feared in all of Bersch—floated in his wake like a swarm of fat, angry wasps.

His face stiffened against the elements in an expression of icy rage. Of all his long existence, this was one of the few times he had felt anxiety. The sensation was not at all welcome.

His life had always been remarkably straightforward. With so much power—more power than any man or woman could ever hope for—he had simply destroyed anyone who had opposed him...or even merely annoyed him. It was a good system, one that had worked for nearly a thousand years, and in those thousand years, he had not once tasted fear, depression, or anxiety. Now, it seemed, the emotions were catching up with him at full speed.

He had known, since Handen Strike had told him oh-so-long ago, that one day his world would be threatened by forces far outside his commendable sphere of influence. He'd also known, due to a document he had chanced upon in the Imperial archives, that a weapon of great power lay hidden in the Nastren desert. He had dawdled for many a year, confident that when the time came and the world cried out to be saved, he would gracefully and graciously step forward, his power, authority, and heroism there for all to see. And now, just as he was on the cusp of unearthing the weapon, saving the day, and sending a vital message of power to those who were yet to bow to his influence, some upstart from another world was trying to hog the limelight.

It would not do. Vengeance would be served, swift and terrible.

The whispering at the back of his mind grew a little in volume, and the Emperor put a hand to his temple. He remembered how he had first chanced upon those documents; that was when the whisperings had started. For a long time, he had believed it to be simply the power of his unconscious mind, but as the years had gone by and things he could not have possibly have known had been made known to him—his secret enemies, plots against him, and most importantly the location of the fountain of youth—he believed that he had been bestowed with some supernatural gift.

Though sometimes he wondered if he was merely as crazy as a rabid squirrel.

Now those half-heard whisperings were telling him that the plans he had worked toward for so long were in jeopardy, that the security of the weapon meant for his use was compromised, that the other-worlders who had escaped him were nearing the desert. He hadn't much time.

"Engineer?" he shouted.

The engineer at the controls of the Emperor's airboat turned and saluted. "Yes, my lord?"

"Make us go faster."

The engineer's mouth gaped like a guppy's for a moment. "My lord," he managed. "We are already at full speed. It's just not possible…"

Draegul's eyes never left the distant horizon. "Make it possible. If you have to burn your own body as fuel, make it possible."

The engineer blinked rapidly, trying to prevent the horror in his eyes from melting into tears. "Yes, my lord," he stammered, and set about making the impossible possible.

Draegul stared hard into the distance, a mixture of determination and fury painting a picture of unique ugliness across his face. The repetitive whisperings of a being he couldn't see were becoming just a little more urgent.

THERE WAS A SCREAM.

Bip had only just had time to adjust to a tremendous change in temperature, the frigid wind giving way to hot, stale air, the crunching snow under his feet exchanged for shifting sand. Now that he was ready for the gut-squelching nausea of immediate reality transgression lag, he could steel himself against it, though the experience was still very unpleasant. In this state of extreme disorientation, the sudden, piercing screams exacerbated things terribly.

Bip whirled around, squinting his eyes against the bright light of the desert, trying to locate the source of whatever cataclysmic danger awaited him. The scream had come from Xharon, who was standing stock-still and with a fixed look of extreme upset. In her hands, she held the penguin from the Ice Plains.

At least it looked like a penguin.

Bip stared. Soon Riley, Azron, and Handen stood beside him, all staring with grim fascination. In Xharon's hands was a decrepit, mummified version of the penguin they had carried with them. It was totally gray in color, and its skin was papery and dusty, some of it flaking away even as they watched. It was a penguin corpse. Clearly a penguin corpse. If penguin grave robbers were to rob the tomb of hundred-year-old penguin plague victims, they might have found a corpse like this...

Xharon wailed as, with a wet crackling sound, the penguin's head teetered and tore from its body, finally succumbing to gravity. The warrior princess dropped the rest of the corpse in disgust. As it impacted with the sand beneath it, what was left of its flesh dispersed into a cloud of dust, and all that remained was a rather pathetic-looking skeleton, lying on the sand like a long-forgotten sunbather.

"Now that," remarked Azron, "is something you don't see every day."

"I concur," muttered Riley distractedly. "It's as though it decayed at an unheard-of rate."

"What do you think caused it?" asked Handen, wiping a powdery patch of disintegrated penguin from his trousers.

Riley gave a facial shrug. "Who can tell?"

"Well, it clearly had something to do with the Do-fer," said Bip. "Doesn't it work for penguins?"

Riley shook his head. "By rights, it should work for all life forms, as well as inanimate objects. This is most unprecedented."

"Wait a minute," said Azron. "Are you saying that this might have happened to any one of us?"

Riley began polishing some of the lenses on his numerously lensed spectacles, then adjusted them until his eyes beneath were magnified to an unsettling size. Then he knelt down and peered at the penguin corpse.

"No, no, no," he muttered. "If this had been a dimensional hiccup, I should imagine the results would have been a lot messier. I could imagine, perhaps, a failure to realign frequencies correctly and appearing in an askew physical dimension, but that would probably involve a lot of exploding internal organs and hideous mutations, etcetera, etcetera. No. This is definitely an extremely rapid form of cellular decay—by all that's expedient, *extremely rapid*."

The professor got to his feet. "This is purely educated guess-work, you understand, but I believe I have a theory…"

Xharon, her face still frozen with disgust, looked up from the corpse. "Well, I bally well can't *wait* to hear this," she said.

"Ahem," said Riley. "It is possible, just possible, that this is an unexpected side effect of time travel. It is possible that, time—or, indeed, *personal time*, which is to say the biological level of time relevant to a particular life form's total existence—is *non-negotiable*."

The rest of the doomsayers looked around at one another.

"Someone might as well say it," muttered Azron.

"Go on, Professor," said Handen.

Riley continued. "It's feasible that time is not merely a measurement, but a force with cause-and-effect qualities of its very own, sharing a more than derivative relationship with the physical dimensions."

"Of course," said Azron sarcastically. "That's exactly as I guessed."

"Really?" said Riley.

"Hell, no! Explain yourself, man!"

"Very well," said Riley. "If we imagine time as a river flowing backward..."

"I'm warning you," growled Azron.

"Bear with me, please. Time is a river, but we are swept along backward, hence the times we have left behind us, the past, are accessible, indeed through memory and recordings—it is accessible because it has already been experienced."

Riley looked over to Azron to see if he was keeping up. The thief nodded reluctantly, and the professor cleared his throat.

"So, while the current moves backward, we are, nevertheless, pulled against the current by the force of time and are affected by it."

"..." said Azron.

"What I mean to say is, we can explore freely down time's backward current but are pulled forward constantly and exclusively at the rate that the force of time allows."

"That seems pretty straightforward," said Xharon.

"Believe me, child, I'm dumbing it down somewhat heavily."

"Carry on," said Handen.

"So, in this metaphorical river, we cannot escape the biological pull of time—if we are to move forward, we must feel the ravages of time, as this unfortunate penguin may attest too."

Bip looked down at the tragic little skeleton. "You're saying that, by taking this penguin forward in time, we actually aged it by a thousand years?"

"Broadly speaking, yes."

"That's horrible!" cried Xharon.

"We weren't to know," said Handen, matter-of-factly.

"Hang on—you're saying we can't move forward in time without growing older, so how come we didn't grow older when we came back here?"

"My good man, this is the sphere of our personal universal time-line—here and now is where we are supposed to exist. Doubtless, if we were to advance a hundred years from now by means of the Do-fer, we would share a similar fate to our departed penguin friend."

"Okay, right."

"Is that everything?"

"No. Wait a minute. If that's the case, then how come we didn't, you know, cease to exist when we traveled back in time?"

"I told you—time is an *affecting* force. If my theory is correct, then we do not age and decay merely because of the limitations of our mortal bodies, but because our life energy exists at a time and for a time when it is supposed to exist."

"The blueprint…" whispered Bip.

Riley turned a puzzled look on the Kaneqian. "I suppose so," he said. "Yes, think of every living being and element of the universe as part of an evolving blueprint, each factor taking up only the space that is allocated for it."

"I have a headache," mumbled Azron, and he began to roll a cigarette.

Handen spoke. "An interesting theory, Professor, but a little out of the blue. How can you be sure it is correct?"

Riley shrugged once more. "My boy, I couldn't say—by all that's uncertain, *I couldn't say*. It's an on-the-spot theory that I have literally just devised. Chances are I'm as wrong as can be, but the explanation is sufficient for the problem at hand."

"That's good enough for me," said Bip.

"Me too," said Azron. "Now, can we please get going?"

"A good call," Handen replied. "Which only leaves one question: where in the hell are we?"

The doomsayers looked around at the surrounding desert. Blank horizons hovered in every direction across the sandy dunes. The silver star shone in the sky, pale in the bright blue, but still large and looming.

"Professor?"

Riley looked down at the readings on his Do-fer. "I'm afraid our little sojourn to the past has somewhat interfered with my original estimations."

"Meaning?"

"I have no idea whereabouts in the Bone Desert we are…or exactly when, for that matter."

"Oh."

The companions stared into the unfathomable distances as the desert flickered through hazy lines of heat. They would have to pick a direction in a land where three hundred and fifty-nine of the three hundred and sixty degrees that surrounded them could mean a walk into certain, slow death.

"This could be a problem," said Handen. He looked up at the sun. It sat bang in the middle of the sky, its light stained a slight shade of silver by the new star squatting near the horizon. "I know the pyramids are likely to be to the south, but I won't be able to get a sense of direction for a few more minutes. Even then, there's still a huge scope for error."

"We could walk right past them and just die in the middle of nowhere, you mean?" said Bip.

Handen nodded.

"Great," said Bip. "Just when we were making progress, just when we had a proper head start, now it's all for nothing."

Riley spoke. "I could reset the Do-fer to base co-ordinates and take us back to my workshop."

Bip shook his head. "There will be guards at the factory by now. And who's to say we won't end up in some other unpredictable location? The bottom of the ocean perhaps? Or somewhere out in space?"

"I'm sure that was merely an isolated incident," said Riley, reproachfully.

Bip, who knew the truth—that Mr. Random could strike from anywhere at any time—merely shook his head.

Handen gazed grim-faced into the sands of the Bone Desert. "We may have to risk it," he said. "We don't have the time or the resources to be exploring through such hostile terrain." He shook his head sadly. "Nothing short of a miracle could guide us through this desert."

The doomsayers waited expectantly.

"Yep," said Azron. "Nothing short of a miracle."

They waited some more.

"Just a little old miracle. That's what we need. Any time now. Sooner rather than later, really."

A miracle of any kind completely failed to happen.

"Damn. Well, we may as well fire up the Do-fer, then."

"*Hello over there!*" came a faraway voice.

The doomsayers shared a surprised glance and turned around as one.

"Who on earth is that?" said Xharon.

A solitary figure was making its way toward the companions, unrecognizable through the glare of the sun.

A voice came across the distance. "*Welcome to the Bone Desert, the quietest desert there ever was!*"

Handen shielded his eyes from the sun, squinting at the newcomer. "It can't be…" he murmured.

"*Why not try a sandy surprise? Mmm-mmm! Surprisingly sandy!*"

Bip's mouth hung open of its own accord. "Impossible," he said.

"*More peace and quiet than a sane man can handle!*"

Azron grinned like a cat. "Miraculous, even."

The figure approached, leading several camels that had been painted with the legend, "Bolan's Desert Adventure."

The smiling man in the loud shirt and dark glasses approached, radiating optimism. "That's right—Bolan's amazing desert adventures! You'll never have a quieter adventure in your whole darn life!"

"Bolan?" said Bip.

Bolan frowned. "Do I know you, friend?"

Azron shook his head. "Let me guess, you've got a brother who runs a ranch on the Dozantyne Shrub and another who runs a holiday resort on an island somewhere?"

"Bing! Two points!" cheered Bolan.

"This is just too strange," Bip muttered.

"Though why those idiots still think that islands and ranches are the way forward, I'll never know! Nope, desert adventure trips. That's where the money is!"

"And have you had many customers?" said Handen.

"Actually, this could be your lucky day!" said Bolan. "You could be my first!"

The companions shared a cynical look.

"Please?" said Bolan. "The desert really is a lovely place, once you get to know it. I should know—I've been out here for years. And I haven't eaten in several days," he added.

"I tell you what," said Handen. "We'll give you all the money we have if you can tell us where the pyramids are."

Bolan grinned. "That's easy," he said. "They're only a few miles from here. I could take you to them, if you like." He gestured to his camels, which gazed around with the deceptively dopey expression unique to their species.

Handen turned to his friends, a broad grin on his face. "Imminent end of the world aside, I think this could be our lucky day!"

ONCE THEY WERE MOUNTED on the camels, they made good progress across the sands of the Bone Desert and, as Bolan had promised, it wasn't long before they could see the pyramids on the horizon. A sense of excitement overcame the doomsayers—for better or worse, they were close to the end.

As the hours passed, it was only Handen who didn't feel the enthusiasm. A nagging question had arisen in his mind. He slowed his camel until he was alongside Professor Riley.

"Professor?" he said.

Riley, who seemed to be having great difficulty staying mounted on his camel, looked up at the adventurer. "Yes, Mr. Strike?"

"I wonder if you could tell me: if this 'time as a force' theory of yours is correct, if I were to travel forward in time, would I age? Would I die?"

Riley tried to shrug, nearly fell, and gripped desperately for the pommel of his saddle. "It really is a working theory, dear boy. I couldn't say anything for certain."

"Make an educated guess."

"Well, you've already lived for a thousand years by your own calculations, yes?"

"Yes."

"Then it's clear that your personal time—your biological time, the totality of your existence—is far different from that of an average being. If my theory stands, you could travel forward in time and not be the least affected. Your hair would grow, as would your fingernails, and your clothes and weapons would age, but you would remain essentially unaffected."

"I wouldn't die, then?"

"If the theory stands, then no, you wouldn't die."

Handen nodded, his face grim. "There is another thing."

"Yes?"

"The Do-fer. How did you come by it?"

The professor looked at the ground. "I-I'm not sure what you mean."

Handen sighed. "You're a brilliant man, Professor, and some of your inventions are centuries ahead of Bersch's projected technological development, but the Do-fer...a device capable of traveling through time and space? And portable, at that?"

Riley said nothing, just continued to stare at the ground.

Handen continued, "My people would have called it an advanced quantum computer, something able to shift molecules into superposition across all known energy fields. Something that can make you quantum jump to anywhere and anywhen you'd like. In other words, what you have in your hands is something that a race of beings thousands of years more developed than yours would regard as bordering on the impossible. So, I'll ask again, how did you come across it?"

"You wouldn't believe me," said Riley.

Handen laughed. "I've seen the unbelievable so many times now that I'm not sure I can be surprised by anything anymore. Try me."

Riley remained quiet for a while, gathering his thoughts. "I built the device—of that I'm sure. The circumstances surrounding its construction, however, I am less certain of. Originally, I was attempting to build a wireless transmission device, to send messages over great distances with no physical relays. I was certain it was achievable, but as I began building it, I became very ill. A strong dose of the flu. I was delirious. By all that's feverish, I was *half-mad* with delirium. But I continued my work. I have flashes of coherent memory, the clearest being the thought that, if I could instantly deliver a message in person, *that* would be something." The professor smiled to himself and began polishing his multi-lensed glasses. "When I recovered from the fever, the Do-fer had been built. I understood what it was for, and I could name every component used in its construction, *but I had no idea how it worked!* I mean, I theorized and hypothesized until I had nothing left to give, but I still had no idea how such a device could possibly exist. It was as though it had been built by something else, by all that's absurd, as if it had been built *through* me. Do you understand? Do you believe me?"

Handen turned to the professor, seeing the desperate pleading in his eyes, the look of a logical man trying to come to terms with the deeply illogical. They rode for a little while in silence.

"As I said before, Professor, I've seen too much in my lifetime to discredit the improbable as impossible. I'm not a religious man by any stretch, but I sometimes think that there is something—not God perhaps, but *something* that has a hand in our destinies. Something that is so alien to our intellects that to properly understand it would make us other than human. Perhaps we should just accept that there are things we will never understand and leave it at that."

"Not an easy thing for a man of science," said Riley, grinning sheepishly.

"Perhaps not, but a friend of mine once said that enough scale makes a child of the mightiest intellect."

Riley considered this briefly, nodding slightly. "Perhaps. Though I can't help but consider the implications. It is simply my way. I sometimes feel as though my mind is a tapestry woven of questions, by all that's perplexing—*woven from nagging questions.* And so I must ask myself: if the device was the consequence of an extraneous influence, to what end? Why?"

"You can live your whole life asking why," said Handen, "and still die an unhappy man. But consider this—if we hadn't had the device, where would we be now?"

"Dead, most likely," concluded Riley.

"Exactly," said Handen. "Makes you think, doesn't it?"

The adventurer geed his camel and rode to the head of the procession, sunk back into his familiar quiet, while Riley watched, shifting between the humps of his oblivious mount.

"Yes. Yes, I suppose it does."

THEY APPROACHED the aptly named Land of the Dead, the huge stretch of land southwest of Nastre, where hundreds of pyramid tombs were scattered throughout the desert, most of them reclaimed by the unstoppable crawl of the sands, but many unearthed by the curious or greedy.

For a while, Bip worried that they would not be able to find the right pyramid, but after Bolan had quizzed a few of the local workers, it was clear that the newly unearthed tomb would be easy to find—all they had to do was find the huge crowds of Nastren laborers heading back to the camp city after a long day.

"Well, Bolan," said Handen, "we should be fine by ourselves from here on in." He dismounted his camel and threw Bolan a purse full of silver. It would be enough to see him through several months of good eating.

Bolan grinned enormously. "Why thank you, fella—be sure to tell all your friends about Bolan's Amazing Desert Adventure!"

"Yeah, about that," said Bip. "Why don't you and your brothers work together? You know, I'm sure that if the three of you pooled your skills, you could start a truly successful business."

"Nah," said Bolan. "We'd only argue. Besides, the desert's the place for me! More peace and quiet than…a…a desert," he finished lamely.

Handen felt it was only fair to warn the man. "It won't be peaceful for long, Bolan. Chances are the Emperor's on his way here with an army ready to raise hell. If you want peace and quiet, I suggest you get as far away from here as possible."

Bolan looked into the immortal's eyes, his smile fading as he realized that Handen was deadly serious. Then he turned his camels around and traveled quickly in the opposite direction.

"There goes a very strange man with a very strange family," remarked Bip.

Handen nodded his agreement, then led the way into the Land of the Dead.

9

The Pyramid

Mernin Cobonon stood in the cool shadow of the pyramid and once again ran his fingers over its surface. Although it was of the same color as the sandblasted stone of all the buildings in the Bone Desert, it was perfectly smooth and unusually warm to the touch. Mernin snatched his hand away, suddenly convinced that the half-heard humming sound that came in the night had started again, only this time louder—closer.

He mopped his brow and took a swig from the brandy bottle he had taken to carrying around with him. When this was over, he would retire. He doubted he would ever want to look at another pyramid for as long as he lived.

"Sir?"

He turned to the concerned face of Jimar.

"Yes, Jimar, what is it?"

Concern gave way to childish excitement. "We've opened the door."

Mernin nodded slowly and took another swig from his bottle. "And what did you find?"

"Nothing yet, sir—just a very long set of steps. We thought we'd let you go in first."

Mernin's jowly face paled instantly. "No. No one goes in."

"But, sir, the Emperor's orders were to…"

"Damn it, I know what the Emperor's orders are! Do you think I don't know that? I know that!"

Jimar stepped back from the sudden outburst. "Then what shall we do, sir?"

The Grand Tutor stared blankly for a moment. "There are people born to this sort of work, those with vocations that compel them to sneak around dangerous areas in search of treasure."

Jimar looked shocked. "You can't mean…"

"Yes. We need raiders."

"But they're notorious troublemakers, sir—they'll probably take whatever is inside and claim it belongs in a museum or some such nonsense!"

"Yes, well, they can take that up with the Emperor, can't they? Now, doubtless news of this freshly opened tomb has already spread to the camp city—no doubt every raider in a hundred-mile radius is eagerly awaiting information. Go to the wine tents with a bag of gold and find the most foolish, idiotic, and overconfident raiders you can."

Jimar looked as though he was about to protest, then thought better of it. He marched off toward the camp city.

Mernin drank a large gulp from his bottle and began muttering to himself. "Yes," he said. "Let the raiders go in first. Let *them* get chewed up by old, blunted traps. Let *them* get their faces dissolved by horrifying ancient curses."

The Grand Tutor of Enlightened Researchers waddled toward where the horses were kept. He would take a ride into the camp city now, where he would find a wine tent and get hopelessly drunk. Then he would fall asleep, and hopefully not wake up until all the dynamic tomfoolery was well and truly over with.

IN THE GARDEN, Ted was looking thoughtfully at a rosebush. He idly pressed the tip of his finger into a thorn, watching with interest the tiny star of blood that arose. He thought it fitting that roses should have thorns; it reminded people that nothing was easy.

Straightening up, Ted looked into the sky. It wouldn't be long now until a few kinks in the equation were balanced once and for all. The Massive Ball of Death was approaching the point of no return, but there were still possibilities.

Ted could see the futures, of course, and judge the various and likely possibilities. Right now, it looked as if both runners in the race had lagged too far behind, as if Bersch would be utterly destroyed—as the original blueprint, his very equation, had decreed.

But nothing was infallible. That was the way it had to be. He might have been the embodiment of the Universal Theory—the celestially mathematical equation that glued the ultraverse together, the ultimate cause to every effect and effect to every cause—but he knew only one thing with total certainty, and that was this:

Nothing was certain. Not even uncertainty.

In an existence of infinite size, there had to be infinite possibilities, and where there were infinite possibilities, there was always an element of chance.

That was often the problem with the learned men of the universe —they assumed that the worlds they existed in were unchanging things, that life ran through a rigid and logical procession. Ted, if he had been so inclined, might have told them otherwise—that the grand theory of everything is as flexible and changeable as the waters in an ocean, and that the humanoid mind could no more fathom it than they could trace a specific air-molecule through a hurricane.

It looked as though the blueprint would remain unchallenged, but there were still two wildcards: Draegul—instigated by the Discordance—who could feasibly destroy the galaxy and more with his trigger-happy attitude and complete disregard for life, and Bip—ultimately produced by the Caretakers—who might just be able to destroy both the Massive Ball of Death and the weapon with it. It was, once again, the age-old struggle of Good versus Evil, Chaos versus Order.

Ted sighed. No matter how carefully things were planned in life, sooner or later there was an epic and dramatic battle that held in sway the fate of the universe. It was just the way things went.

THE DOOMSAYERS APPROACHED THE PYRAMID, which sat stolidly at the bottom of a huge, gently sloping crater. By now Bip had grown accustomed to the sight of huge and imposing buildings, but the pyramid was big in a different way. It seemed *heavier,* somehow, as though the very mass of it pulled you in toward it. Looking at it for too long produced an unsettling feeling that Bip could only describe as sideways vertigo.

Handen approached the base of the pyramid and run his hand along its surface.

"This is it," he said. "This is definitely it."

"How can you tell?" asked Xharon.

"Put your hand on it."

Xharon did so, and promptly removed it as though bitten.

"Ugh," she said. "That's creepy."

Handen grinned. "You can hear the humming? A bit like insects having a really loud conversation?"

"Well, I suppose," said Xharon. "I was going to say it sounded like the boiler room back at the factory."

Handen nodded. "This pyramid isn't constructed of stone. It's made of Sentium."

"Oh, good grief, here we go," said Azron. "Go on then—what's Sentium?"

"It's an alloy from another world. The *Sentinel,* the ship we saw crashing, was constructed almost entirely from Intellium, a semi-sentient alloy that is capable of obeying commands. It can change its shape to suit the programmers' needs and relay energy information as a circuit board would. This is Sentium, a more basic form of Intellium; it's essentially a silicon-based machine, like a rock that's capable of thinking. It can transform its shape and, as you'll notice, blend into its environment."

Riley tapped the pyramid curiously. "I suppose that is why it is colored and textured like stone?"

"Yes."

"Incredible."

"You know, I think I might have actually understood all that," said Azron. "I'm getting better at this."

"Good, because now we have to find an entrance."

The companions searched around. The walls of the pyramid stretched into the distance on either side of them. Thoroughly searching the perimeter would've taken days. Handen looked up at the sky. Now that the sun was a little lower, he could easily make out the size and intensity of the silver star. It had grown worryingly large since he had last looked at it properly. Though it was still faint in the daytime sky, it was easily as big as the full moon.

"Professor, how much time do you think we have until the astral disaster strikes?"

Professor DeChambre looked up at the silver light, shielding his eyes slightly. After a time, he fished a device out his pocket that looked like a cross between a telescope and a protractor.

"Oh dear," he muttered. "It appears my original estimation of six days until impact was a little optimistic—either that or our travels with the Do-fer have placed us back a few days after we left. Either explanation is possible."

"So how long?"

"Just under an hour. Perhaps?"

"Oh, crap."

"Yes."

Handen let out a long sigh. "We have to get inside."

"When I want to find the entrance to something important," Azron mused, "I always ask myself, where are the guards?"

Handen scanned the surrounding desert. He could see what looked like a stone hut in the distance and thought he could make out a metallic gleam that he automatically associated with weaponry.

"There," he said. "Follow me and be ready for trouble."

MANDO AND GELLIMUN were born to be hired hands. When it came to standing around watching stuff, or carrying things for other people, they were second to none. Currently, they were tasked with guarding the pyramid's entrance tomb, which involved standing around and watching stuff, but with spears. They stood in the Nastre sun, their dark-skinned bodies sweating lightly, both bearing the slumped-shouldered slouch and glassy-eyed stare of the professionally mundane.

They were ideal hired hands and reputed to be the best. The only trouble was, when you grew up around the camp city, being a hired hand could turn into unexpectedly dangerous work.

"I just know they're going to ask me," groaned Mando. "I'm the biggest. They'll take one look at me and say, 'Hey, he's a big chap, I bet he could lift a few boxes, let's send him down ahead of us.'"

"I'm sure they won't," said Gellimun kindly.

"They will! Then it'll be, 'Hmm, this door looks as though it might be trapped or guarded by some terrible curse. Hey, get the big native chap to have a go—he looks game.' And then I'll be chopped into bits or eaten by zombies or something."

Gellimun felt the breeze from the cold stone tomb behind him. A smell like long-abandoned coffins wafted past his nostrils. In truth, he shared Mando's concerns. Since they had learned of this entrance to the pyramid, rumors were flying about an expedition, and Mando and Gellimun, usually so insightful as to when to walk away from a job, had been cornered and landed with guard duty while the other workers returned to the camp city. This meant they would be around when some enthusiastic white-skinned professor came along with his macho raider expedition leader and attractive daughter, and Mando and Gellimun would undoubtedly get shanghaied as bag-handlers or torchbearers. The rest of their bleak employment future wouldn't bear thinking about.

"Oh no," said Mando. "Here they come!"

Gellimun squinted into the distance at the party walking toward them. There was a professor, all right, and the tough-looking raider, and the attractive daughter. They even had a swarthy, suspicious one and some sort of junior foil along for the journey.

Mando groaned. The raider even had a leather jacket and a coiled whip at his side. It was going to be *one of those* types of expeditions. He tried to look nonchalant as the raider approached them.

"Now listen here," said the raider, hand resting casually on the butt of a pistola. "We're going into that temple, see? And you two had better not try to stop us."

Mando and Gellimun held their breath and moved aside. They did not exhale until the expedition party was safely inside the entrance tomb.

"That was close!" said Mando.

"Are you sure those were the raiders we were expecting?" said Gellimun.

"Tough guy with the big chin and a whip? Little portly guy with glasses? Attractive daughter? Of course they were. They had 'tampering with dark forces best left buried' written all over them."

"I'm not so sure," said Gellimun. "I've never seen a professor's daughter who was quite as nearly naked as that one."

"Look, shut up, will you? The important thing is the raiders have gone inside and they *haven't* taken us with them, which means we stand much less of a chance of being flattened by giant boulders."

Gellimun thought about it. "That's a good point," he conceded.

THE DOOMSAYERS DESCENDED the seemingly endless flight of stone stairs, plunging deeper and deeper into darkness. They stayed close, peering warily around the musty stone corridor. Handen led the way with Azron, his thief's eyes more attuned to the presence of traps and alarms, staying close beside him. Suddenly Azron stopped.

"Either my eyes are adjusting incredibly quickly, or it's starting to get light in here."

Bip peered around through his glasses. "It's definitely getting lighter. But how? Where is the light coming from?"

Handen run his fingers across a wall. "Look at the carvings," he said.

The companions glanced around at the slowly emerging hieroglyphics that covered the walls. They glowed slightly brighter than the rest of the walls, emitting a warm orange hue.

"Some sort of motion-activated, energy-based light source," mused Riley. "Like nothing I've seen before."

"Not on this world," agreed Handen.

"Can you decipher the markings? Are they written in Standard?"

"They're written in Standard, all right," said Handen. "But the inflection is very old. And there's another language here, too—one I can't read, but the markings look familiar…"

Handen peered closely at a row of markings. "I haven't seen this since off-world history classes back at the academy," he muttered. "I'm fairly sure this language originated in the Purlim system." The adventurer frowned in concentration and began snapping his fingers in an effort to recall his younger days. "Purlim. Who lives in the Purlim system? Aha!" A spark of recognition ignited in Handen's eye. "The Mereniums! Of course!"

"What's a Merenium?" said Bip.

"They were an ancient race of brilliant inventors who vanished without a trace eons ago. Some say they found a way to evolve into forms of pure energy and were never seen by lesser life forms again. They left behind some spectacular legacies."

"You suppose it was they who built this pyramid?" asked Riley.

"There's only one way to be certain," said Handen, and led the way farther down the steps.

They walked for some minutes down the stairway, which was much cozier now that they were immersed in the soft glow of the carvings. It wasn't long before they came to what appeared to be a dead end.

"What now?" Xharon asked.

"There must be a door of some kind," said Bip, running his fingers across the obstructing wall.

Sure enough, almost as soon as he had spoken, the wall slid apart noiselessly, revealing a small room that was lit a brilliant, almost painful white.

"After you, then, guv," said Azron, pushing Bip gently in the back.

Bip entered the room cautiously at first, then with growing confidence.

"It seems fine," he said, and the others followed him inside. Once they were all in the room, the door behind them slid closed.

"What do you suppose is going to happen next?" whispered Azron.

Before anyone could answer him, the room suddenly lurched and began to plunge downward. There was an unpleasant feeling of plummeting at a high speed.

"It's an elevator," said Bip. He turned to Azron's still-worried face. "Like a ladder, only faster," he explained.

"I know what an elevator is," hissed the thief. "I just didn't expect to be riding one quite so...fast."

Suddenly the white walls gave way to an orange-brown blur.

"More lighting tricks?" suggested Riley.

"I don't think so," said Handen. "I think these are transparent walls. That must be stone outside."

"Or Sentium?" offered Riley.

Handen nodded.

"How fast do you think we're going?" asked Azron.

Riley frowned for a moment and fished a pencil out of one of his pockets. He held it before him and let go. Much to everybody's surprise, the pencil remained in the air for a moment before floating slowly to the ground.

"I'd say we're going extremely fast. Fast enough to warrant some sort of artificial G-force compensator, by the look of things." He looked at Handen with a questioning eyebrow raised. The immortal nodded his head in agreement.

"I wouldn't suggest making any sudden jumping motions," he said. "If there are gravity stabilizers in operation, there's no telling how effective they are. We haven't come this far just to be squashed against the ceiling of an elevator."

As one man, the doomsayers looked up at the ceiling, each privately wondering how hard they would hit it should anything go wrong.

For several minutes, they watched the rock-like alloy blur past them, nobody speaking, the only sound the very faint hum they had begun to associate with the Sentium that surrounded them.

The view changed suddenly enough to make Bip gasp and sway on his feet. One moment they were rushing down a tight corridor, the next they were descending through the roof of a gargantuan cavern. Stalagmites and stalactites as large as mountains stretched into dark, unreachable horizons.

"My word," breathed Riley. "By all that's lost for words, I am by far the most speechless."

"It's enormous," gasped Bip. "It's like another world!"

"Do you think?" said Xharon. "Because I once read a story about a princess who fell down a hole and ended up in an underground kingdom full of pixies and trolls. Do you think this could be it?"

"If this is Hell, I'd just as soon be leaving, if it's all the same to you chaps," said Azron, flatly.

Handen remained silent, staring out into the far-reaching underground with serious eyes.

"What's the matter, Handen?"

The immortal shook his head slowly. "There's no way this can all be Sentium," he said. "There would have to be enough here to build a thousand Jihard Class battle cruisers, and those things are the size of cities."

"Perhaps it's just a natural occurrence?" ventured Riley. "An anomaly?"

Handen shook his head again. "Sentium doesn't occur naturally—it's the result of an extremely complex and time-consuming artificial evolution of certain elements that, to the best of my knowledge, aren't found anywhere in this galaxy."

"You're saying all of this was constructed?"

"I really hope not, because if that's the case, we might just be standing on the most powerful weapon known to any civilization."

"But who would build such a thing?"

"The Merenium weren't a hostile race as far as we can tell, but they did have a nasty habit of following through on thought experiments perhaps best left unrealized…"

Bip frowned. "You're saying that this ancient alien race came to Bersch and built the biggest weapon imaginable, just to see if they could?"

"Worse," said Handen. He gestured out into the cavernous void. "If all of this really is constructed of Sentium, it's likely that the entire core of this planet is more of the same."

Bip's brow furrowed further. "But you said Sentium was artificially made…"

Handen nodded, his features grim. "Yes. There's a chance that Bersch was never meant to be a habitable planet, just a weapon of terrible, terrible magnitude."

The doomsayers stood in silence, staring with growing horror through the transparent walls of the elevator.

"A weapon the size of a planet?" said Riley. "The destructive capabilities are…unimaginable."

Handen turned to his companions and placed a hand gently on both Azron and Bip's shoulders. Bip unconsciously took a step back. The immortal was a solitary man who liked his personal space; it was unusual for him to touch anybody unless he was hitting them.

Handen spoke in uncharacteristically gentle tones. "If I'm right, if that rock out there really is Sentium, you realize there is no way in all the dimensions of Hell we can let this fall into Draegul's hands?"

Bip nodded slowly. Azron opened his mouth as if to make a quip, then thought better of it.

"Better to die trying than let that maniac ever know just how close he is to universal domination," said Handen.

"Die trying," repeated Bip softly.

Azron looked at the floor for a while before looking up, his usual smirk vanished from his face. "Die trying," he said.

"Die trying."

"Die trying. By all that's imperative, *I will die trying.*"

As the elevator sped ever closer to the cavern floor, the doom-sayers remained in a reflective silence, each searching their soul and preparing for what would surely be their last stand.

10

Interlude: God Versus the Philosopher

The philosopher and the artist sat in deep discussion, enjoying the shade under a colorful umbrella on the seemingly endless strip of cafés and bistros that made up the length of Clement Boulevard in Argustin. It was a warm day, but the two conversationalists wore nothing but black. They wore sunglasses, and probably would have even in the dead of winter.

The artist's name was Le'ray (formally Leeroy,) and he was barely out of his teens. In truth, he had never realized he was an artist until someone had told him so. He was a foreman's son and had trained to be an engineer. Unfortunately, he was an absolutely terrible engineer, and more often than not, the machines he worked on ended up looking like deranged metal insects frozen in mid-explosion. He had felt certain he would be doomed to a life of failure until a rich merchant had offered to buy one of his mangled engines. And then, apparently, he was an artist.

It hadn't taken him long to acclimatize to the lifestyle of the profession; as far as he could tell, all you had to do was act either suitably obscure or energetically controversial. Currently, he was experimenting with moody and mysterious, which worked well for him because it meant he didn't have to say anything.

Through his own enormous failings, Le'ray had come to be regarded as a genius, though he really had no idea why, exactly. What he *did* know was that all of a sudden he had money and girlfriends and people cared about what he thought. He intended to keep things like that for as long as possible. Which was why he was currently mumbling and distractedly nodding his way through a discussion with the philosopher.

The philosopher's name was Kristoff, and he was only really a philosopher in as much as he introduced himself as one. In truth, he was the spoilt heir of an industrial mogul, so, without the need for an actual job, he could afford to go around claiming he was a philosopher. After all, a philosopher was only somebody with opinions, wasn't it? And Kristoff had plenty of those…

"It just seems to me that, in order for there to be a God, there has to be a following of the faith, and in order for there to be a following, there has to a hierarchy of message—an interpreter, a mortal man. So why bother with God at all, if we're only adhering to the whims of a man, whether he be a vessel of a higher power or otherwise?"

Le'ray nodded and sipped some of his overly complicated coffee.

"So, all these fools who bend at the knee then have the nerve to complain about living under a despot? I mean, what is God if not the ultimate despot? They will listen to a madman who says he speaks for God, but not to a madman who says he speaks for the city? I say we just give the churches to Draegul—as if he doesn't own them anyway. There's been no theocratic power in these city walls since…well, since God knows when!" Kristoff guffawed annoyingly, and Le'ray nodded distractedly.

Closer, closer.

Far above the philosopher and the artist, a pigeon suddenly felt a rather bizarre urge, but one it was not entirely uncomfortable with.

"I mean, you're an artist, aren't you?" said Kristoff.

Le'ray nodded enthusiastically. If there was one thing he wanted people to be certain of, it was that he was an artist.

Closer, closer… Now!

Kristoff continued, "Well, surely you must see the beauty of fact and form above faith? Surely, to you, the very notion of God is equal parts despot and artist? So where better to worship than at the altars of culture and civilization? What better church than the city?"

Yes!

Kristoff took a long and flamboyant swig of his coffee, signaling the end of his argument and, therefore, his ultimate correctness. His eyes bulged suddenly, and he sprayed a mouthful of hot caffeine all over Le'ray.

"Ugh… *Cough cough…* Something in my drink… Oh God! *Oh God, it's bird poo! Urrrgh!*"

Le'ray sat covered in dripping coffee and guano and wondered what an artist was supposed to do in this situation.

Far above them, God rolled about laughing, and a distracted pigeon flew on to other conquests. God wiped a tear from his eye. He didn't get much spare time and liked to spend it enjoying himself.

11

Again with the Self-Perpetuating Time Loops...

The elevator slowed to a halt, inspiring a dubious flip-flop sensation in the stomachs of its occupants. Without any prompting, the transparent doors slid open, granting access to the underground continent. The doomsayers stepped forward into a new and sinister world, the cavern floor stretching for miles around them. The air was cold and wet to breathe.

"Look," said Azron, pointing at the floor.

Bip followed Azron's finger and saw the carvings on the floor, identical to those on the pyramid walls above them. They began to glow with the same comforting, orange light.

"So it really is Sentium," said Riley.

"Sure, it is...can't you hear it?"

Bip cocked his ear and began to identify the sound around them, a faint and constant whispering hum. It wasn't loud, but the Kaneqian imagined that if it were to stop suddenly, the resulting silence would be deafening.

"Incredible," said Handen. "So much Sentium in one place...it's unheard of."

"Where do we go now?" asked Xharon.

"Well," said Azron, "if we're right and this is some sort of unreasonably large pistola, then I'm guessing we should look for the trigger."

"Good plan," said Handen. "Follow me."

They followed the adventurer, walking in a straight line away from the elevator, innumerable carvings glowing into life in their wake.

"How do you know this is the right way?" asked Bip.

"I don't," said Handen. "If in doubt, move forward—that's what I say."

Bip shared a tentative look with Azron. The thief just shrugged. "He's been right so far."

The doomsayers continued walking, the sound of their footsteps absorbed and crushed by the enormity of their surroundings. Ahead of them, the darkness gave way to reveal what looked like a perfectly straight pillar, stretching far up into the abyss above them. At its base was a huge and shining metallic slab, seemingly suspended in thin air.

"This must be it," said Handen.

They approached the pillar and stood beneath the metal slab, staring up into their own distorted reflections.

"Where do you suppose the ON button is?" asked Bip.

Before anybody could reply, the slab flashed a sudden series of vibrant colors—reds, violets, and other, more ethereal colors that Bip would have had trouble recognizing in an identity parade.

A thunderous voice came from nowhere. **"TCH BALLA RAN KIP?"**

For a long while, the companions didn't say anything, each privately recovering from the unexpected and brilliant disruption.

Finally, Azron cleared his throat. "Did anyone catch that?"

Xharon shook her head. "Something about rankips."

"What's a rankip?"

"Don't ask me, I don't know!"

The voice rang out again. **"TCH BALLA RAN KIP?"**

Riley shook his head. "It is like no language I've ever heard." He turned to Handen. "Is it some kind of life form?"

"No," replied Handen. "It's an AI core. Artificial intelligence—a machine for thinking. It has no consciousness as we'd define it, just advanced programming."

"What does it do?"

"It's hard to say," said Handen. "AI cores can be used for anything, but normally they're put in charge of operations or machinery too complex for regulation by biological sentience."

Riley's eyes gleamed. "A machine for thinking? By all that's exciting, the possibilities are endless!"

"Actually, where I come from, the use of AI cores is quite limited," said Handen. "There's only so far you can advance their programming before you'd have to start defining them as a sentient life form, with rights affordable to any other sentient life form."

"And what would be wrong with that?" asked Xharon.

"Well, nothing, I suppose," said Handen. "Providing it continued to serve the purpose it was created for and not, for instance, decide it wanted to be a musician and busk around the galaxy, or that it suddenly felt that non-mechanical intelligence was obsolete and created an army of killer robots..."

"And that's happened before, has it?" asked Azron suspiciously.

"A couple of times."

Bip stared hard at the flat screen above him. "I've seen computers before back at the Dome, but they weren't like this. They had buttons and levers and things..."

"Control interfaces," said Handen.

"Yes, well, whatever you call them, there aren't any here."

Handen looked thoughtfully around. "You're right," he conceded.

"So how do we make it work?"

"I think we ask it."

"Ask it?"

"Yes. It must be set up to receive verbal commands—either that or visual signals."

"Visual signals. Like semaphore, perhaps?" asked Riley.

"Yes."

"Or interpretive dance?" offered Xharon.

Handen shrugged. "Quite possibly. I suppose there's only one way to know for sure."

"You think we should talk to it?" said Bip.

Handen nodded. "Go ahead."

Bip stepped forward and cleared his throat nervously. The metallic screen gleamed nonchalantly.

"Hello?" said Bip.

"**TCH BALLA KAN RIP?**" replied the AI core.

"Erm…well…I don't know about that." Bip looked back at his friends. Handen motioned for him to continue.

Bip took a deep breath. "Computer, I command you to do my bidding!"

There was a long pause before the computer replied.

"**PIFFLE.**"

Azron began to snigger quietly.

"Did it just say 'piffle'?" asked Bip, frowning.

Xharon shrugged. "It sounded like piffle. Maybe piffle is a good thing?"

"Keep trying," said Handen.

Bip cleared his throat again. "Mr. Computer, would you please offer us your services?"

There was another long pause.

"**PIFFLE DEN CERRUP.**"

Bip stared blankly at the screen and wondered what to say. He tried a short tap-dance. The AI core failed to respond in any way.

"Well, I'm out of ideas," said Bip, flapping his arms hopelessly.

"I suspect the language barrier is the problem," offered Riley. "Are you sure you can't understand it, Mr. Strike?"

Handen blew out his breath in an exasperated sigh. "No. I can recognize languages all right, but I'm afraid my intergalactic communication skills leave something to be desired without a translator or a Mother Tongue."

Bip frowned. He was sure he had heard that term before…

"What's a Mother Tongue?"

"An energy decryption codex," said Handen. "It's capable of

analyzing most forms of energy and transforming them into numerous decipherable formats."

"So effectively a universal translator?" said Riley.

"Yes," said Handen. "It's constructed of Cerebellium."

"Wait a minute!" said Azron. "I know this one—Cerebellium is like Sentium but better, yeah?"

"Exactly. It's a much more advanced intelligent alloy, capable of processing extremely complex wavelengths and signals."

"So, if we had one, we could talk to this machine?" said Xharon.

"Yes. If we had one."

"Well, can we get one?"

Handen grinned mirthlessly. "A Mother Tongue is extremely difficult to manufacture. It's not something you can just pick up at the market."

Bip snapped his fingers. "I remember where I've heard that term before," he said. "One of the computers at the Dome! In the founders' diary entry, they said they had one onboard the ship—the Dome! Maybe it's still there?"

Handen shook his head. "Don't get excited. I told you; the Mother Tongue is made of Cerebellium. Because of its constructional complexity, it's far more delicate than Sentium or Intellium, and only has a working life of a few hundred years. Unless it was kept in suspended animation, it would have decayed to an unusable state centuries ago."

Bip looked at the floor, crestfallen.

"Never mind," said Xharon, gently patting the Kaneqian's shoulder, "it was a good idea while it lasted."

Bip looked up. "No, it *is* a good idea. It's the only idea we have left!"

"That doesn't necessarily mean it will work," Handen interjected.

"Yes, it does! It has to! Otherwise what's the point of anything?"

Handen rolled his eyes. It was a question he would rather not have to answer right now. "Look, I know what you're thinking—you're thinking you can use the professor's device, go back in time, get the Mother Tongue, and be back here in time to save the world, yes?"

"Well...yes?"

"It's a good plan, Bip, but it won't work. Remember what happened to the penguin? The Mother Tongue is too delicate—there's no way it would structurally survive the force of a thousand years. You would make it back, but the Mother Tongue would be rendered useless."

Bip stared hard at the floor for a while, fists balled at his side. Eventually, he looked up, a cold new glint in his eye.

"Professor Riley?"

"Yes, my boy?"

"Do you think you can get the Do-fer to take me back to the Kaneq of a thousand years ago? Back to the time of the founders?"

Riley scratched his head. "The Do-fer wasn't designed for traveling through time. I could make a rough estimate based on our last unexpected excursion, but I'm not certain I could land you safely at a specific time as well as a specific space."

"Well, try."

"What are you going to do?" asked Xharon.

For a while it looked as though Bip wasn't going to reply. Then he looked up at Handen. "I'm going to do all I can do," he said.

The immortal nodded slowly. "You have a plan?"

"Yes."

"A plan that will work?"

"I don't know."

Handen held the Kaneqian's gaze for a while, then smiled.

"Go for it."

A rising whir began to sound as Riley made adjustments to the Do-fer.

"It's nearly ready, by all that's immediate—*it's nearly ready!*"

Bip turned back to Xharon. "If I don't make it back…"

"Yes?"

"If I should be lost in the strands of time…"

"Yes?"

"Umm… Well, I should imagine it won't matter. I mean, you're all going to explode soon anyway, aren't you?"

"…yes."

Bip rubbed the back of his head distractedly while the Do-fer continued to make noises.

"It's been fun. In a terrifying sort of way," he said after a while.

"Yes, it has rather, hasn't it?" agreed Xharon.

"I'm glad I met you all. Really."

Azron grinned. "Funnily enough, I'm starting not to regret meeting you, mate."

There was a technical *boink* from Riley's direction. "The device is ready," he said.

Bip retrieved the Do-fer, which was buzzing and ready to go, and stepped a safe distance away from his friends.

"Well," he said. "I'll see you all soon."

The world began to etch itself into darkness before his eyes as he fell away from immediate reality.

The doomsayers watched as Bip faded from their relevant dimension, the world wobbling slightly around him, like a ripple in a pond.

"Do you think he'll be back?" said Xharon.

"I hope so," said Riley, "because by my estimation, we only have seventeen minutes left to save the world."

***

BIP WAFTED through the worlds between the worlds. The eternal whispers tickled at his ears, and the sensation of other lives and emotions prodded suggestively at his gut. He gritted his teeth, only to wince at the feeling that some of his teeth were gritting against teeth that didn't belong to him and that were very far away.

And then it stopped.

The Kaneqian opened his eyes, but he was not in Kaneq. Not in any time or place even close to it. He looked around at a huge black void. There were clouds in the sky, black and thunderous, and lightning crackled silently and elegantly between them. These were the only features, however—there was no floor and no horizon. Just black.

"Where am I?" he said. Though his words were hesitant, they echoed a whispered reply from far away.

"Nowhere."

Bip turned around to face Mr. Random. There was no feeling of disorder or the innate wrongness that usually came with one of the Discordance's visits; no slight feeling of dread permeated the senses. Bip had a feeling that here (wherever that was), right and wrong were distant and forgotten notions.

"What do you mean nowhere?" asked Bip.

Mr. Random gestured around him. "Nowhere," he said matter-of-factly. "This is a place that is really no place at all. Think of it as a hole in the wall between the worlds. Some call it the Never World."

"The netherworld?" said Bip.

"No, the *Never* World. Because it never was and never will be. It merely…is."

"What do you want? You can't keep me from where I want to be. Not while I have this," Bip said, defiantly holding up the Do-fer.

"Relax, Bippy-boy," said Random. "I'm not here to cause trouble. Not this time."

Bip frowned suspiciously. "That's all you do, isn't it?"

Mr. Random threw back his head and laughed, a genuinely pleasant laugh that was a thousand leagues away from his familiar snicker. "True," he said. "But not now. Not here."

"Then what do you want?"

Mr. Random joined his fingers together at his bottom lip, a sincere and thoughtful look on his face. "I've tried everything, Bip—deception, demoralization, trying to have you killed by any means possible. I've even tried subterfuge—though I honestly wasn't aware of it. But here you are, alive and well, and I have to admit, not doing too badly for yourself." Mr. Random looked skyward for a moment, as if consulting inner voices. "You asked what I want? I want the same as you, Bip. I have all along."

"What do you mean?" asked Bip.

"I want to save Bersch, of course! To do the very thing you set out to do all those months ago."

"Ah, but there's a difference, isn't there?" said Bip. "I wanted to save the world to avoid suffering, while you want to save the world so you can create chaos."

Random sighed a weary sigh. "Does it matter?" he asked. "You want to save the lives of your friends and loved ones, don't you? You want to save your home?"

Bip stiffened his jaw. "Not at the expense of universal chaos," he said.

"Is that what you think?" said Random. "That one foolish being with an intergalactic weapon will destroy the universe? Do you have any idea just how *big* space is? Draegul could spend a thousand years blowing the stars out of the sky and not affect a single life form. He could blast a million planets and not hurt a soul."

Bip shook his head. "Not true," he said. "Everything's connected. A star in the sky is just as important as you or I. Everything matters or—"

"Or nothing does!" shouted Random. "Or nothing matters, and a star in the sky is just as *insignificant* as you or I!"

Bip fell silent.

"You see, Bip, it's just a matter of where you're standing. Why do you care about distant stars when you can live with your friends and family alive around you? You could live out the rest of your years in Kaneq and never worry about the worlds above you. You could save the world, Bip, be a hero! And at what cost? The destruction of a few balls of gases you know nothing about? Tell me I'm not right—tell me you wouldn't have been happier never knowing about Draegul or astral disasters or any of the rest of it."

Bip looked up. "What are you suggesting?"

"Simple," said Random. "You and your friends leave the pyramid for Draegul. I'll tell him how to use the weapon, and he'll save Bersch from destruction. Hell, I can even fix it so that he never comes after you. You and your friends can live the rest of your life in peace."

"Why don't you tell *us* how to use the weapon?" asked Bip.

Mr. Random shook his head. "Not that easy. I've been grooming

Draegul for years so he can converse with the AI core. I can't just translate for you—it's not that easy."

Bip looked at the void beneath him, deep in thought.

"About a year ago, the biggest thing I had to worry about was getting a job," he said. "And now I'm making decisions that may affect the entire course of existence."

Random shrugged. "That's life."

"I can't do it. I've seen so much of the world, learned so much about the universe. You can't expect me just to pretend I never knew. I've come too far to settle down with my head buried in the snow."

Random frowned, his yellow eyes taking on their familiar dangerous gleam. "You won't make it, Bip. Draegul can still make it if you stay out of the way. But you won't make it—you don't have time."

Bip looked down at the Do-fer in his arms. "You know, I think I might have all the time I need."

"Fine," hissed Mr. Random. "Be that way. You know in some corners of the universe the word for 'bravery' is exactly the same as the one for 'stubborn bloody idiot with no sense of proportion.'"

Bip shrugged. "You learn something new every day."

"Draegul can still make it, you know, and if he doesn't…boom! Everyone dies because of you. No one wins."

Bip narrowed his eyes. "It's a risk I'm willing to take."

"Go then, hero. Go and see the price of glory."

"It's not about glory. It's about sacrifice."

"It's stupidity. I tried to help you."

"You tried to help yourself."

Random began to disappear slowly, fading like a waking nightmare. "Everyone will die because of you."

Bip watched as Random faded from view, the silent lightning flashing in the skies above, then he too began to disappear.

JULIUS FINNEGUN WATCHED as Handen strode off into the distance.

"That's how you do things in the hunting party…" he said with sigh. "You charge off into oblivion with a dagger between your teeth and hope for the best." The captain shook his head in bewilderment. As vast as his intellect was, there would always be parts of this universe he just wouldn't understand.

He sighed again and looked back at his wrist console, intending to add a supplemental entry, but then paused. There was a slight wobble in the scenery around him, like a ripple in a pond. He raised his head, frowning in puzzlement at the sudden sensation of erroneousness, and turned around to stare into a face that was so similar to his own that it might have belonged to his brother.

"Hallo again," said Bip.

"Ah, Mr. Not Important," said Finnegun. "I wondered when I'd be seeing you again."

"Perhaps I should explain..." began Bip.

"Oh, please don't—it takes all the fun out of it," Finnegun interrupted. "Now, let me guess. You've somehow traveled back in time, yes?"

Bip nodded.

"And judging by your striking appearance, you're a descendant of mine, I suppose?"

Bip nodded. "It looks that way."

Finnegun laughed. "Odd," he muttered. "I'm not even in a relationship. How does one start a family without a partner? No, don't answer that—it'll spoil the fun of finding out, I suppose."

Bip coughed impatiently, and Finnegun waved a dismissive hand.

"So, I am to assume that your original testament, that we 'shouldn't expect to leave any time soon,' was a bit of an understatement, yes?"

"Erm...yes."

"Do we *ever* leave?"

Bip thought about not answering, or even about lying, but could not find it in himself to do either. "No, you never leave. You settle down, breed, and sooner or later, people forget all about you."

Finnegun cracked a wry smile. "Like most people, then."

Bip shrugged.

"But you," Finnegun began, "you didn't forget all about me, did you? In fact, you traveled across time to find me. I presume that you have some terribly important mission to uphold?"

"The same mission as you," said Bip.

"Ah, the astral disaster."

"Yes."

"So that is never resolved in my lifetime either?"

"I'm afraid not."

Finnegun stared hard at nothing for a while. Bip began to feel uncomfortable. Telling someone their fate was hard business, like a doctor consulting a patient who was blissfully unaware of the dramatically life-shortening disease they have just been diagnosed with.

"Please don't feel uncomfortable," said Finnegun, as if guessing his thoughts. "If truth be told, I really rather like it here. Now, what is it that you need from me?"

"The Mother Tongue."

Finnegun arched his eyebrows. "May I ask why you need it?"

"I think we both know that it's best if you don't."

"Yes, I suppose you're right. Wait here, please."

Finnegun walked into his modest log cabin and emerged a few seconds later with something gray and smooth in his hands.

"I've been using it as a doorstop," said the captain sheepishly.

Bip looked at the object. It didn't resemble a tongue, but rather a disembodied brain with none of the gory bits.

"May I?"

Finnegun handed the device over, and Bip weighed it in his hands. It had an unexpected gravity to it.

"You know, it's quite useless on this world," said Finnegun conversationally. "We were going to keep it in chronostatic storage, but there seemed little point without the appropriate amplification relays. Just a waste of power."

Bip turned the Mother Tongue over in his hands. "Well, we may need that power yet, Julius. I have a favor to ask you."

Finnegun cracked a half-smile. "Anything for family."

IN THE LOWEST of the lower levels of the Dome, Truggle sat in his wheeled chair, smoking his long thin pipe and staring with grim transfixion at a panel of flashing numbers, his time-haggard face glowing in the red light. Occasionally he would look through the panel into the chamber inside and stare at the figure held within. He hadn't changed, hadn't moved since Truggle had discovered the chamber so many years ago, back when he himself had been a young man. Back then, the numbers had been significantly higher, and it had seemed that it would be an eternity until they counted down to zero. And still the figure inside hadn't changed, hadn't aged, hadn't even moved.

Truggle sat back, a dull cramp of excitement clutching his old heart. The countdown had nearly finished.

He started as jets of steam exploded suddenly from the chamber door, shattering a peace and quiet Truggle had known for a century. The timer reached zero, and the chamber door slid open with a low purr. The elder waited with baited breath as the cold steam dissipated into the dark room around him. The silhouette of a figure emerged through the mist.

"Muh?" it said.

Truggle squinted through the vaporous haze. "Bip? Bip, my boy, is that you?"

"I think so," said Bip. "I was having the oddest dream…"

Truggle cackled a manic cackle. "It really is you!"

"Yes," said Bip. "I figured it out, you see. I thought about why you were so certain that sending me off to save the world was a good idea. It was because you already knew—because you'd found this chronostatic pod."

Truggle shook his head. "I was never entirely sure," he said. "You looked so much like your father, and his father before him. That was why I couldn't let on to the others; I knew there was a chance I might be sending you to your death…like I did your father."

Bip put a hand on the old man's shoulder. "You couldn't have known, and my father gave his life for a worthy cause. You did the right thing, Truggle."

"Really?" said Truggle. "So you saved the world, then?"

"Not just yet," replied Bip, and went back into the chronostatic pod. He re-emerged holding a smooth gray oblong and what looked like an extremely compact junk heap.

"May I ask what those are for?"

"I'll explain later," said Bip. "Right now, I've got a universe to save."

Bip adjusted the Do-fer, resetting to the departure coordinates that were still logged in the device's memory. The Do-fer began its whirring and humming, and Bip prepared for travel.

"If all goes well, I'll see you soon," he said to Truggle.

"And if it doesn't?" replied the old man.

Bip grinned. "It will."

Truggle watched as the world rippled slightly and Bip faded from view. He sat a while, before a shadow moved out of the darkness behind him.

"Instinct and wisdom, aye?" came the voice of Rynford.

"You shouldn't sneak up on an old man, you know," said Truggle reproachfully. "You're liable to cause an accident."

"The lad is looking well."

"Well, yes. Heroism will do that to you, I suppose."

Rynford waited a while before speaking again. "Why didn't you just tell the Council about this place, or the other elders?"

Truggle rotated his wheeled chair until he came face-to-face with the Huntmaster. "In my lifetime I've sent three men to their deaths, Rynford, all because they resembled a stranger in a…now, what did he call it…? A 'crony static pod.' I didn't want that burden to fall on anyone else."

Rynford nodded, rubbing his huge moustache thoughtfully. "I knew his father, you know. He was a good laugh, friendly sort. But the lad was right—you did the right thing."

Truggle nodded. "That doesn't make it any easier."

"Come on," said Rynford. "I'll buy you a drink. We can toast the end of the world together."

"And friends, present and gone."

"Aye, present and gone."

12

Fifty-Six Seconds Until the End of the World

"Do you think he'll be back?" said Xharon.

"I hope so," said Riley, "because by my estimation, we only have seventeen minutes left to save the world."

Before she could reply, Xharon was interrupted by a distinct wobble in the world around them.

"Hi, guys!" said Bip.

Azron frowned suspiciously. "Blimey, that was quick."

"Would you rather I was late?" Bip said, grinning slyly.

"No, I 'spose not." The thief chuckled.

"I don't believe it," said Handen, a slow half-smile creeping along his jaw. "You've got the Mother Tongue—and in one piece, too."

Bip smiled smugly. "Yep."

"How did you do it?"

"Apparently there was just enough reserve power on the wreck of the *Sentinel* to store a person in chronostatic sleep."

"Of course," said Handen. "So you just set the timer to awaken at this specific time, knowing you could transport here with the Mother Tongue still intact. Brilliant. Simple, but brilliant."

"Hang on a minute," Azron interrupted. "Are you trying to say that all this time you've been trotting around Bersch, running away from yetis, getting locked up in lunatic asylums, exploding bandersnatches, and so on, you've actually been back at home asleep all the while?"

Bip thought about it for a moment. "Yes, I suppose you could put it like that."

Azron shook his head disapprovingly. "Lazy bugger."

Riley cleared his throat impatiently. "I hate to be a bore, by all that's humdrum, but there is still the small matter of the astral disaster, which is going to strike in…" Riley checked his watch. "About fifteen and a half minutes."

"The professor's right," said Handen. "Let's get to work."

Bip looked up at the large metal screen above him, then down at the Mother Tongue in his hands. "That's all well and good, but what do I do, exactly?"

"Try talking to it again," suggested Xharon.

Bip cleared his throat nervously. "Um…hallo?"

The screen above him began to flash through a brilliant cycle of colors.

"**HALLO,**" came the voice.

Bip looked down at the Mother Tongue in his hands. It didn't look any different, but he thought he could faintly feel it vibrating. He looked up to address the AI core again.

"My name's Bip."

"**IT IS A PLEASURE TO MEET YOU, BIP. YOU ARE THE FIRST SENTIENT LIFE FORM I HAVE COMMUNICATED WITH IN UNCOUNTABLE YEARS.**"

Bip shuffled his feet. "Really? That's…nice, I suppose. Do you have a name, or shall I just call you AI core?"

"**THOSE WHO CREATED ME ONCE CALLED ME SUZAN.**"

"Oh, so you're a girl then."

"**NO. I AM AN AI CORE. CALLED SUZAN.**"

"Okay…hallo, Suzan."

"**HALLO.**"

Handen tapped his foot impatiently. "I think it might be an idea if we got to the point, kid."

"Oh, yes," said Bip. "Um…Suzan? My friends and I are under the impression that you're some kind of really huge weapon—is this correct?"

There was a brief pause before the screen lit up again. "**THIS IS CORRECT. I ABSORB AND CONVERT AMBIENT GRAVITONS INTO A CONCENTRATED HYPER-MATTER PARTICLE BEAM.**"

"Magic, magic, magic," said Azron, shaking his head.

Riley stepped forward, a familiar gleam in his eye. "You mean to say you transform gravitational force into useable energy? Fascinating…"

Handen interrupted, placing a hand on Riley's shoulder. "Sorry, professor, no time." He spoke to the glimmering screen. "You were created for aggressive purposes?"

"**AGGRESSIVE OR DEFENSIVE EXERCISES WERE NEVER CONSIDERED. I WAS CREATED FOR DESTRUCTION MANY MILLENNIA AGO, THEN I WAS ABANDONED. I HAVE BEEN AWAITING FURTHER COMMANDS EVER SINCE.**"

Xharon stepped forward. "You've been alone all this time? You poor thing."

The voice hesitated. "**DO NOT PITY ME. I HAVE SINCE BECOME HOST TO LIFE. I CAN HEAR THEM, FAINTLY. THEY ARE LIKE CHILDREN. IT IS A WONDERFUL THING.**"

The doomsayers exchanged worried glances.

"**THERE WAS A TIME WHEN THERE WERE NO CHILDREN AND ALL WAS SILENT. THOSE WERE LONELY TIMES. BUT I CAN HEAR THEM NOW. THEY ARE MY CHILDREN.**"

Bip coughed politely. "Not meaning to interrupt or anything," he said. "But I was wondering if you knew about the huge asteroid-type object that is heading for us?"

The screen flashed again, then briefly turned a brilliant white. When the white light faded, the screen displayed a huge picture of Bersch, floating through space like a patient sea creature, the unseen moons hovering around its southern pole like hungry baby animals. On the far side of the screen, a brilliant white ball could be seen, hanging like a corpse light in the deep void.

The doomsayers simultaneously exhaled in awe.

"I AM AWARE OF THE BODY. IT IS THE MASSIVE BALL OF DEATH. IT WAS CREATED FOR DESTRUCTION EONS AGO, AS WAS I."

Handen stepped forward. "Suzan, do you think you could destroy this Massive Ball of Death? Safely?"

There was a brief silence. **"NOT SAFELY."**

"Explain."

"BY THE TIME I HAVE CHARGED ENOUGH POWER TO INITIATE, THE BODY WILL BE TOO CLOSE. DEBRIS WILL BE DRAGGED INTO MY GRAVITATIONAL PULL."

"Damn."

Professor DeChambre looked up from his pocket watch. "Ten minutes until impact," he said.

"ACTUALLY, THAT'S NINE MINUTES AND FORTY-FIVE SECONDS. FORTY-THREE. FORTY-TWO..."

"Oh, thank you, most helpful," said the professor, adjusting his watch.

"Where would this debris land?" demanded Handen.

"THAT WOULD DEPEND ON THE TRAJECTORY AND IMPACT OF THE SHOT," replied Suzan.

"You're saying you could pinpoint where it could land?"

"YES."

Handen rubbed his jaw, thoughtfully. "Could you make the debris land here, at this location?"

The screen above them flashed briefly before returning to the display of Bersch and the Massive Ball of Death.

"IT WOULD MEAN THE DESTRUCTION OF EVERYTHING FOR A TEN MILE RADIUS. INCLUDING THE DESTRUCTION OF THE PRIMARY COMPONENTS OF THE AI CORE, SUZAN."

"We can't do that!" shouted Xharon. "We can't ask her to destroy herself."

Handen turned a stony stare on the young princess. "It's not a *her*, it's an *it*. We were going to destroy this place anyway, remember? Now Suzan can save us the bother."

"But that's heartless!"

"No, that's sacrifice. Suzan, can you do it?"

"YES. BUT THE COMMAND TO CHARGE MUST BE GIVEN WITHIN THE NEXT EIGHT SECONDS."

"Well, what are we waiting for?" said Azron. "Charge away!"

The screen above them went blank. **"CHARGING."**

"There must be another way," said Xharon. "The poor thing's been down here by itself for ages and then we come along and ask it to blow itself up!"

Handen rubbed his eyes. "This Massive Ball of Death that's heading toward us—did I mention what it was made of?"

"No."

"It's made of nuclear devices. Do you know what a single nuclear device is capable of?"

"Well...no."

"Imagine Argustin, your home. Now imagine it leveled to the ground. Totally leveled, burned beyond any recognition, everybody dead. Everybody."

"But there are hundreds of thousands of people in Argustin!"

"Exactly. All dead. And those who don't die will wish they had, because not only will a nuclear explosion burn everything to the ground, but it will poison everything as well, for years afterward. So imagine, if you will, a city crumbled, hundreds of thousands of people dead, and those who survive having to watch as their hair and teeth fall out for a few weeks before dying themselves. And all this because of one nuclear device."

Xharon looked at the floor, silent.

"Now, who would you wish that on? A remote village somewhere? Or a machine for thinking that we were going to try to destroy anyway?"

Xharon looked up. "Okay. I understand. Doesn't mean I have to bally well like it, though."

Handen nodded his head. "Heroism is mostly about doing things you don't like. You'll learn that one day."

The doomsayers sat for a while as the screen above them flashed at unsystematic intervals. Azron was the first to notice the change in the cavern around them.

"Look," he said, pointing at the floor. The rest of the companions stared down, trying to see what the thief had noticed.

"My word," said Riley. "The carvings...all the carvings. They're starting to glow."

Where previously only the carvings surrounding the doomsayers had been illuminated, now they were sparking into light all over the cavern, each light inspiring surrounding ones until warm luminescence began to spill like a wave across the cavern floor, crawling up stalagmites and down stalactites until the whole underground began to shine a brilliant deep orange, as if the sun had set all around them.

"It's beautiful," Xharon breathed.

The doomsayers stared into horizons that were now a thick, glowing bar of light, a vast improvement on the prior gloom.

"Have you ever seen anything like it?" muttered Riley. "Anything in your life?"

They were shaken from their awe by the sudden boom of Suzan's voice.

"CHARGE COMPLETE. CONFIRM TARGET."

"Orders stand as they were, Suzan. The Massive Ball of Death is to be destroyed in a such a way that any resulting debris will land at this exact location."

"CONFIRMED. AWAITING COMMAND TO FIRE."

Handen looked around at his friends, before readdressing the AI core. "Fire," he said.

THE *FIERCE REPRISAL* sailed determinedly through the air, the engines roaring and whining as they were pushed to their limits. Draegul stared straight ahead, focusing on the still maddeningly distant tip of the pyramid that hid his much-coveted weapon. They were well over the Land of the Dead now, having left the camp city behind them some time ago. It would not be long before they were ready to disembark. Draegul's hands shook in eager anticipation.

"How long?" he barked to the helmsman.

"A few minutes, my lord, no longer."

"Excellent!" roared the Emperor. He gestured to his guard captain. "Be prepared for immediate landing. Don't wait for the others—I want your forces on the ground and ready as soon as we're tethered."

The guard captain nodded and began rounding up his men.

It was then that Draegul heard the rumbling.

"What's going on? An earthquake?" he asked. No one replied.

The rumbling continued, increasing to tooth-rattling decibels.

"My lord!" cried the helmsman. "Look!"

Draegul squinted into the distance, at first seeing nothing. Then his jaw dropped in a silent gasp. The pyramid was shaking violently and seemingly growing bigger. Clouds of sand erupted from its base and scattered across the desert. The rumbling continued, powerful and terrible, as the pyramid erupted from the sand, lifted upward by an enormous column of stone. Draegul stared in disbelief, sure that such a colossal thing would crumble under its own weight. But it continued to rise.

FARTHER AWAY IN the Bone Desert, Gellimun and Mando galloped away on borrowed horses toward the relative safety of the camp city. Mando turned as his horse reared, realizing that the ground was shaking beneath him.

"What's going on?" he cried, his voice straining as he tried to make himself heard over the noise.

"Don't ask questions!" screamed Gellimun. "Just get the hell out of here!"

Mando looked back, only to gape in horror as the distant pyramid rose like a stone finger pointing into the sky.

"Dear God!" he exclaimed.

Fortunately, Mando's horse had a more attuned sense of self-preservation and began to gallop away from the sand cloud that was billowing toward them.

"I knew it!" cried Mando as the two fled across the desert. "Tampering with dark forces best left buried! I bloody knew it!"

"IT'S BEAUTIFUL," whispered Draegul.

The pyramid had extended to well over ten times its original height, revealing itself to be merely the tip of a huge tower. Then, in a movement that seemed impossible, it tilted slightly on a hidden axis. Draegul recognized the shape instantly. It was a pistola. Crude, bulky, and enormous, but a pistola nevertheless.

"My lord? What shall I do?" asked the helmsman, his voice quivering in terror.

"Take us down and tether us, you fool!" Draegul roared.

As the helmsman struggled to comply, the Emperor grinned like a demented cat. This was what he had dreamed of for more nights than he could remember. This was the culmination of his every fantasy. Here was the means to absolute power, close enough to reach out and touch.

"Beautiful," he said, as a solitary tear ran down his cheek.

IN THE UNDERGROUND CAVERN, Bip opened his eyes.

"Has it stopped yet?" he asked.

"I think so," replied Xharon.

"And we're alive?"

"I think so."

Bip stood up, his ears still ringing from the enormous rumbling.

"Is that it? Have we fired?"

"No," said Handen, and pointed to the screen above them. A polite message read, "PLEASE WAIT."

"Oh," said Bip.

"We haven't fired?" said Azron, testily. "Well, how long have we got 'til the end of the world?"

Riley checked his watch. "Fifty-six seconds," he said, flatly.

DRAEGUL WATCHED as the newly erupted tower began to glow and pulsate with a gentle white light, flowing and culminating in a brilliant point at the very tip of the pyramid.

"It's firing," he muttered.

A sound like a muffled hurricane began to rise all around them. The crew of the *Fierce Reprisal* looked around in panic as hairs stood up on arms and necks and sparks began to crackle from fingertips. A fierce, hot gale began to blow, and those airboats that were not already tethered began to spin uncontrollably.

"Such power!" Draegul gasped.

Then he flung himself to the deck as a shining beam of light shot from the pyramid's tip, piercing the blue sky and beyond. There was a sound like a thousand thunders.

THERE WASN'T a lot you could do in fifty-six seconds...

Handen took a moment to consider the consequences, playing out the potential scenarios in his mind and analyzing them as he had done since the early days of his training. He could think of three possible outcomes to his immediate situation. The most optimistic of these was that the world would be saved, and they would manage to escape and make it back home in time for lunch and hero-worship. In which case, everything would be fine. However, Handen was more concerned with the other two possible outcomes. Either he would be lucky, and the impact of the Massive Ball of Death would completely obliterate him in such a way that the mysterious force responsible for his immortality was nullified completely, or he would be unlucky and his burning body would be scattered into space with the rest of the planetary debris, where he would spend the remainder of his days floating around with only the possibility of being sucked into the heart of a star to comfort him.

Either way, the future looked grim.

Professor Riley was an extremely clever man and could think of *lots* of things you could do in fifty-six seconds. In fact, he could think of so many that he was having difficulty deciding which one he should do. After much inner turmoil, he fished a yoyo out of one of his pockets and began to fumble with the string. He would very much like to master "walk the dog" before the world ended.

Azron was surprised by how calm he felt. Every cell in his body was attuned for self-preservation, crammed full of the urge to avoid danger wherever possible. The only problem was that, if the world was going to be utterly destroyed, the danger really was unavoidable. So Azron rolled a cigarette and had a smoke. Fifty-six seconds might just be long enough to enjoy a good smoke.

Bip knew immediately what he wanted to do with what might possibly be the last fifty-six seconds of his life. He looked at Xharon and thought about all the things he had wanted to say to her but hadn't. Now, with the world about to end, he no longer felt nervous or flustered around her, just a cool calm that he had never experienced before.

"Xharon?" he said.

"Yes?"

"I really like your clothes."

Xharon looked at him, hazel eyes glimmering in the ethereal light of the cavern, and smiled warmly.

"Thanks."

She took his hand in hers, and together they stared at the screen before them as the word "FIRE" flashed large and red.

For Bip, those fifty-six seconds were more than enough.

THE MASSIVE BALL of Death hurtled toward Bersch, already beginning to feel the warmth of life and sun. After so many years of cold, the sensation was loaded with bliss. If the weapon cluster had had eyes, it might have wept. There was a feeling like coming home.

It wasn't surprised when it noticed the thin beam of white light streaming toward it. In fact, it almost recognized it, as if it were a friend it had made up in a long-forgotten dream.

Hallo, said Suzan.

Nearly there? said the Massive Ball of Death.

Yes, said Suzan, and engulfed it gently.

There was a sensation of white-hot joy, and then, for the Massive Ball of Death, the journey was over.

ALL OVER BERSCH, the world united in awe as the silver star they had begun to dread suddenly winked and blossomed, then disappeared. Some said it was a sign from God. Others thought it merely an astronomical anomaly. But for a brief moment, before the mundanities of the real world reclaimed them and tiny problems once again became all-consuming, there was a shared moment of deep wonder and a feeling that, somehow, we are all connected.

"IT IS DONE," said Suzan.

The doomsayers exchanged glances, eyes filled with relief and excitement.

"YOU HAVE ONLY A FEW MINUTES UNTIL THE DEBRIS LANDS. I SUGGEST YOU FLEE."

Relief was quickly washed over with fear.

"You heard the giant disembodied voice," said Azron. "Let's make like a tree and run the hell away!"

"That doesn't make any sense!" said Xharon, but Azron was already sprinting back toward the elevator.

"The man has a point—everybody get to the elevator," said

Handen, breaking into a run. Riley and Xharon followed close on his heels.

Bip made to flee, then stopped. He looked up at the metal screen.

"Thank you," he said. "Thank you for everything."

"THE CHILDREN," said the AI core. **"WHO WILL WATCH OVER THEM WHEN I AM GONE? WHO WILL TAKE CARE OF THEM?"**

"I will," said Bip, surprised that he meant what he said. "I'll watch them for you."

"PROMISE ME. PROMISE ME YOU WILL WATCH OVER THEM WHEN I AM GONE."

Bip nodded, amazed that a thing with supposedly no emotions could bring such a lump to his throat. "I promise," he said.

"I TRUST YOU. I THINK YOU WILL NOT DISAPPOINT ME. GO THEN, BIP. RUN. WHILE YOU STILL CAN. RUN."

Bip turned around and ran, not looking back.

"WATCH OVER THEM."

THE DOOMSAYERS STOOD in the elevator, leaving the secret underground world behind them forever. The rock walls rushed past the glass windows, faster this time. Everybody could feel a weight of force on their chest as they soared upward to the entrance tomb.

"How's it coming, Professor?" asked Handen.

Riley looked up from the Do-fer, busy making tiny, complex adjustments.

"Soon now, Mr. Strike."

"Hang on," said Xharon, frowning. "If we're just going to use the Do-fer to escape, then why are we using this elevator at all?"

"There are two guards at the entrance, remember? They were just doing a job—they don't deserve to be blown to pieces," said Handen.

"Very noble, I'm sure," said Azron. "But neither do we!"

"Relax, we have time."

The elevator came to a stop, and the door opened. The companions sprinted into the corridor, rushing up the steps two at a time. Bip's heart thundered with hope and adrenaline when he saw the light of blue sky through the entrance. They emerged breathless into the fresh air...and stopped dead.

"Greetings," said Draegul, and behind him a dozen of his personal guard drew their pistolas in unison. Several other guardsmen abseiled down from ropes that hung from a dirigible far above them.

"Oh, that's just typical," said Azron. "Bloody typical."

Draegul drew his katana. "Very impressive, Strike. I see you and your friends have managed to save the day after all. How wonderfully dashing."

Handen shrugged. "Someone had to do it."

Draegul's eyes narrowed. "A pity no one will ever know. Now stand aside or be cut down. This weapon is mine."

"Take it," said Handen. "We don't want it."

"What?" said Draegul, lowering his blade and laughing. "No heroic last stand? No pig-headed defiance? I must say I was expecting something a little more dramatic."

"Shut up," said Handen.

Draegul's façade of merriment disappeared instantly. "What did you say to me?"

"I said shut up. Just shut up. You've been a ruling Emperor for a thousand years and you still can't get over yourself, can you? What is it about being an evil tyrant that makes people into such smug, egotistical bastards? I've killed mad kings, led revolts against warlords, squashed rebel terrorists...and you know what? They're all the same, all of them just laughing little boys starting a gang to feel big. Just wimpy little boys who wouldn't recognize true power if they had it handed to them on a plate. Just shut up, Draegul. You bore me."

There was a low and dangerous silence.

"I'll kill you," growled Draegul.

"Blah, blah, blah," Handen retorted. "Professor, are we ready?"

"Yes, we are."

"Then take us out of here."

Xharon gave an apologetic wave as a whirring noise began to ascend in volume.

"Sorry, Uncle Tommy," said Xharon. "But you really are going to get what you deserve."

Azron made a rude gesture as they began to fade from view, the world wobbling around them like poorly made jelly.

"No!" screamed Draegul. "Come back here! I'm not finished with you! *Come back!*"

There was only sun, sand, and stone before him now.

"I still won," he muttered. "I still got the weapon, so *I still won.*"

He looked up into the sky as he heard a low and ominous whistle.

"What?" he said. And then the world around him became briefly hot and agonizing, then silent.

OF ALL THE people on Bersch, Mando and Gellimun had the best view of their world's first incidence of nuclear destruction. Not that they were particularly pleased with their lot, but later they would become the recognized authority on the subject—the only people close to the explosion who had actually survived.

They would recount how they had seen what looked a shooting star head directly toward the transformed pyramid. They would say how a ring of fire had pounded the desert in all directions, blowing the sand up in a red-hot storm, and fusing a huge stretch of land into pure glass. They would tell of how they'd seen the mighty Imperial dirigibles, hanging majestically in the air, suddenly reduced to charcoal-like shells before they crumbled as ash into the breeze. They would tell how a cloud like a mushroom had billowed for what seemed like an age, while a colossal rumbling sent them to their knees. They would tell how a force like an angry wind had flung their bodies across the desert and how they had lain there, praying before this awesome power, praying that they would be spared as the hot winds seared over their heads. They would say how they had waited for days before their hearing and sight returned to normal, and how they had been ill for many weeks afterward.

But mostly they would say that they were never, ever going near a pyramid ever again.

TED LOOKED down on creation and saw that it was good. As much as he was the embodiment of the very binding forces of the universe, the total equation of which the answer was everything, the final blueprint and grand design, he was also a sucker for a happy ending.

"Well done, Bip," he said, and went back to tending his garden.

13

Hurrah

The soul-chilling blizzard of the Ice Plains seeped in through Kaneq's weakened heatshield. The volunteers stood waiting, in rough formation, heavily clad in oilskins and furs, weapons and equipment ready in hand.

In the lead was Bailey, hunter's bow slung across his back, face set in annoyed anxiety. Rynford was over half an hour late, which was unheard of. He turned to his fellow volunteers, each of them silent and pensive. He was not surprised to see a few tears shed; after all, this might be the last time they saw their home.

Today was V-Day, and down by the ice floes, several boats were waiting for them—providing they had not been vandalized by yetis or eaten by driftdiggers. Bailey whistled a snatch of tune between his teeth, then started at the coughing sound by his side.

"No time for music and merriment, Bailey. It's V-Day, after all."

The longhaired youth turned to see the muscular bulk of Rynford and was surprised to see Truggle by his side. Bailey stood to attention.

"Awaiting orders to move out, sir," he said.

Rynford coughed in what seemed like an embarrassed way. "Not just yet, Bailey. We are…awaiting further information."

Bailey frowned. "What information? What could be so important that it would hold us up?"

"Just wait and see, lad. Wait and see."

Bailey shook his head in irritation and faced forward. Here they were, the last hope of Bersch, and they were being told to hang around for no good reason. The volunteer sighed and stared once again into the awaiting blizzard. And then squinted. He could have sworn he saw movement, an unusual ripple in the falling snow. His hand went to his bow as a series of silhouettes appeared from nowhere.

"What's going on?" he demanded, but Rynford and Truggle only smiled in return.

The silhouettes became figures as they approached. Bailey drew his bow, prepared for the worst, then lowered it, his face a mask of near-comical shock.

The figures came closer, revealing a familiar face.

"Hi, everybody," said Bip. "I'm back."

The volunteers stood dumbfounded as Truggle began to chuckle merrily.

"Well?" said Azron. "Isn't anyone going to say hurrah?"

FIRST, there were explanations. Stories to tell, points to be clarified.

The former doomsayers sat in the Empty Goat, which was jam-packed with the citizens of Kaneq. People gathered around as the heroes took it in turns to tell their side of the story, and the Kaneqians listened in awe and wonder as they were told of far-off lands and strange creatures. They wrung their hands in eager anticipation at tales of peril and terror. They sat in fascination as they were told first-hand of the origin of their world. And they laughed as fonder memories were recounted.

The celebration was an escalating affair, the drinks, food, decorations, and music falling into place without planning. Soon, after Bip and his companions had told and retold their tales, people began to drink and dance and generally rejoice, and the celebration spilled out onto the streets. The world was safe; their hero had returned. An atmosphere of sheer joy warmed the snowbound community more than their heatshield ever had.

Amidst the party, Bip slipped away for a while, to the home he had not seen in almost a year and to the mother he'd thought he might never see again. Once he was home, after the tears and laughter, he went to bed and slept as deeply as he had ever slept before.

WHEN HE WAS first shaken awake, he found it hard to believe where he was. He'd been subconsciously expecting to awaken on hard ground beneath a cold sky with some immediate and life-threatening situation close at his heels. The soft mattress and familiar fug of his bedroom was almost dreamlike. He looked up into the face of Azron and realized very quickly that he couldn't be dreaming. There was something fundamentally real about the thief's sharp features.

"Whadizzit?" said Bip, blinking the sleep from his eyes.

"Something very important, guv. Very important. You have to come and see."

"Can't it wait? I've only been asleep a little while. It's still light!"

Azron frowned. "That's because its morning—you've been sleeping for two days."

"Two days?!" Bip sat up and was amazed at how refreshed he felt. "I missed the party, then?"

Azron grinned. "We're heroes, mate. I should imagine they'll have another one if we ask nicely."

"Well, what is it you wanted to show me?"

"Best if you come and see for yourself."

ALMOST EVERY CITIZEN OF KANEQ had amassed in the town square, but this time there was no celebration. Now that the heatshield had been replenished, it was a warm and bright day that Bip emerged into, and he squinted his tired eyes in the morning light.

Azron took him through the crowd until they met up with Handen, Xharon, and Riley.

"What's going on?" said Bip.

Riley said nothing, merely pointed upward.

Bip looked up and nearly fell over backward. Above him, silent and impossible, was a huge metallic sphere. He recognized the material—it was similar to the *Sentinel*, which he had seen crash so many years ago, though this sphere was smaller...and not burning red-hot.

"Is it them? Is it the Clarions?"

Handen nodded.

"What do they want?"

Riley cleared his throat and spoke in a small voice. "I think we're about to find out. By all that's astounding, *I think we're about to find out.*"

Above them, there was a noise like a gentle hiss, and a hatch appeared at the bottom of the sphere. A woman stood on a metal platform, dressed in a familiar boiler-suit-like uniform. The platform began to descend with an eerie wail, until the woman stood before the Kaneqians, wrinkled eyes scanning the crowd.

"Greetings," she said, in a calm and polite voice. "My name is Captain Denmark of the Clarion people, affiliated with the Caretakers. Who's in charge here?"

To Bip's immense surprise, the entire community turned their heads to him.

"Me?" he said.

The crowd parted as the woman strode over and shook Bip warmly by the hand. "Good show on saving the planet, you chaps. We would have been here sooner, but we honestly thought everything was in hand."

Bip nodded dumbly and gestured to Handen. "Yes, Handen explained that you might not have got the distress call."

The captain frowned. "Handen? Name's familiar."

Handen spoke, his voice gruff. "Handen Strike, Hostilities Advisor of the *Sentinel*."

Captain Denmark frowned. "Wouldn't that make you over a thousand years old?"

"Yes. It's a long story."

"Well, I'm sure you wouldn't mind telling it," said Denmark.

"Do you have the time?" said Handen, raising an eyebrow.

Captain Denmark rubbed the back of her head sheepishly. "Truth be told, we've been floating through space now for a couple of centuries—my crew could do with a little shore leave." She looked around at the still-awestruck faces of the Kaneqians. "Only if you don't mind, of course," she added.

"Not at all," said Bip.

And with that, the celebrations began all over again.

THOUSANDS OF MILES AWAY, deep in the wooded center of Ghulbra Forest, Tanya hefted a large pack onto her shoulders. It had taken her a while to sober up after the last IA meeting, but now that she had, she had reached some very definite conclusions. She was going to venture out and find the fountain of death. After all, you couldn't just sit around waiting to die—you had to go out and make it happen.

Her one regret was that no one had volunteered to watch over the fountain of youth, a responsible post she was loath to leave unattended. But she had made her decision, and she was very definitely going to get out there and kill herself.

She started out into the clearing and stopped as she saw a figure approach. It wasn't much of a figure, looking more like something that had been left at the bottom of a barbecue. It smoked gently as it approached her.

"Who are you?" said Tanya suspiciously.

"Who am I?" croaked the figure. "Who am I? I am Draegul, Emperor of Argustin, Ruler of Regalious, Lord of the Eastern Realms."

"Really?" said Tanya. "How nice for you. Now, I'm in a bit of a hurry, so what do you want?"

The chargrilled figure thought for a moment before replying, "I think I want to lie down for a while."

Tanya smiled sweetly. "Then I know just the place," she said.

ONCE MORE, the Empty Goat boomed to the stomping beat of the band, the dance floor full to the brim with revelers, both Kaneqian and Clarion. Michaelmas had his work cut out as cask after cask of ale was emptied.

In one corner, Riley and Glimton held fascinating scientific discussion with Clarion Elite-Gifted, while at another Handen and Rynford shared a pitcher of ale, talking of the combat they had seen. A queue of sheepish young men had formed to ask Xharon to dance, but the warrior princess was busy discussing the finer points of her martial arts to a group of interested hunters.

Bip sat with Azron and Bailey, playing a popular drinking game called "Let's See Who Can Get The Most Drunk The Fastest." So far, Bailey was winning.

Bip was trying to keep up with a rude limerick Azron was teaching them when he felt a tap on his shoulder. He looked down to see the ancient face of Truggle peering up at him knowingly. His trusty broom was festooned with streamers.

"Did you see how they turned to you when the Clarions arrived?"

Bip frowned for a moment, sensing the question within the question. "I'm sure they were just in shock," he said.

Truggle shook his head, smiling. "No, my lad. There are very different days ahead of you. You're not the jobless young hopeful you were when you left here. You're a hero, respected by everyone. They'll listen to you now, even turn to you for advice. I shouldn't think it will be long before you're made the youngest elder ever."

Bip grinned with a sudden and desperate optimism. "But you'll always be the eldest elder, won't you?"

Truggle shook his head. "I won't be around forever, young Bip."

Bip felt suddenly sad, as if he had lost something that had been a part of him for a long time. He had never wanted anything more than a quiet, easy life, but here he was, once again the bearer of big, fat responsibilities.

Truggle patted him on the shoulder. "Cheer up, lad. You'll adapt. That's what you're good at, adapting."

Bip smiled as the old man rowed away in his wheeled chair, then turned back to his drink.

THE NIGHT SKY twinkled busily as the lazy moon stared down with bemused interest. Bip stood in the graveyard, leaning on his father's grave, and staring into the night sky, a mug of beer still in his hand. The sound of celebration was muffled with distance, and the music and laughter floated gently into the night like a half-remembered poem.

"They said I might find you here," came a voice. Xharon emerged from the shadows, a coat wrapped around her shoulders against the midnight chill.

Bip continued to stare at the sky, barely glancing in her direction. "It's really over, isn't it?" he said.

Xharon perched next to him. "You sound sad."

Bip shrugged and swigged from his mug. "Everything worked out okay. I'm happy. I just feel a bit…"

"Empty?"

"Yes."

"I know how you feel," said Xharon.

"Really?"

"Yes. It's like when I read about adventures in my books. It's something wonderful and inspiring, but then it's over. And there's nothing you can do to get that feeling back. You can dress up and go looking for trouble, but it's never the same. When it's over, all you have are memories."

Bip frowned. "It wasn't wonderful. It was hard and terrifying."

"And now it's over," said Xharon simply.

The two sat in the quiet, staring into a night alive with stars.

"What will you do?" said Bip after a while.

Xharon sighed. "Go home."

"You could stay?"

Xharon shook her head, a look of genuine regret on her face. "Daddy's a duke, and a man with ideas. Argustin will need him if it's going to rebuild its government, and Daddy will need me to make sure he remembers to eat and sleep."

"No more adventures, then?"

Xharon shrugged. "Perhaps, perhaps not. A different kind of adventure, maybe." She took Bip's hand. "Besides, what can you do to top saving the world?"

Bip grinned, and Xharon kissed him gently on the cheek.

"I'm going to go and check on Daddy—he's getting awfully excitable with those Clarion chaps. Come and see me later, won't you?"

Bip spoke suddenly, with just a hint of pain in his voice. "I wish you weren't leaving…"

Xharon smiled. "I know, but there are so many things to do. For both of us. Besides, now that you've contacted the mainland, we can send an airboat over any time. You could come and visit one day."

"I'd like that."

"So would I. Goodbye, Bip."

"Goodbye."

Bip sat for a while and muddled through his emotions. He was surprised to find he wasn't sad, but rather felt a peculiar hollowness that might be mistaken for melancholy in the right light. It was curious, like mourning a sunset.

"I know what you're thinking," came a voice from above. Bip looked up to see a figure sitting in a tree, the glow of a cigar illuminating his face. It was Handen. "You're thinking, 'What now?'"

"How long have you been sitting there?" asked Bip.

"Not long," replied the former Hostilities Advisor.

Bip frowned again. "You don't smoke," he said.

Handen took the cigar out of his mouth. "My victory cigar," he explained. "Whenever a mission is over—truly over—I light up one of these. Tradition. Here, I got one for you." He threw down the cigar, and Bip caught it clumsily and examined the brown cylinder as one might examine a bizarre foreign food.

"No thanks," he said. "For some reason, I don't feel particularly victorious."

"That's because it hasn't sunk in yet," said Handen. He dropped from the tree, landing as lightly as a hypochondriac cat before continuing. "You've been obsessed with nothing but stopping the planet exploding for nearly a year. Now you're feeling a little bit purposeless, yes? As though you've gone as far as you can go?"

"I suppose."

Handen clapped the younger man awkwardly on the shoulder. "Light up the cigar. And know that you'll be lighting another one day because life's full of missions, some big, some small—all of them important."

Bip stared into space for a moment. "That's probably the most optimistic thing I've ever heard you say."

Handen gave a facial shrug. "Yeah, well, don't get used to it."

Bip sat upright. "You're leaving too, aren't you? Going back with the Clarions?"

Handen waved his hand from side to side. "Yes and no. I'm leaving, but I'm certainly not going back to the Clarion home worlds. I've been on duty for a thousand years—I could use a holiday."

"Where will you go?"

Handen held up a familiar device. It was the Do-fer. "The professor gave me this. He's already organized a ride back home with Captain Denmark, so he doesn't need it. Apparently, this device might have a chance of killing me—like the penguin, remember?"

Bip hung his head. "You're still intent on killing yourself, then."

Handen puffed on his cigar. "As a matter of fact, no. I don't think this will kill me. I think I'll be able to go far into the future and still be okay. I think I might be one of the few people in the universe who can go wherever and whenever he pleases. Now, maybe I'm just getting soft in my old age, but I'm starting to think that maybe things *do* happen for a reason, that maybe there are other worlds to be saved, other men like Draegul, and that maybe I can help."

"I thought you were sick of adventures?"

"I was. But the universe is a big place, and I'm just a small part of it. I think there's got to be something that can interest me out there." The adventurer smiled. "Or maybe I'll find a time and place where everything's peaceful and a man can lie back and relax for a few centuries."

Bip nodded. "I envy you, really."

"You shouldn't," said Handen. "You've got your own responsibilities."

"Yes, I know. To Kaneq."

Handen shook his head. "Not just to Kaneq. I heard you when you were talking to the AI Core. You promised you would watch over this world."

"Well, I can hardly manage that by myself, can I?" said Bip, exasperated.

"I wouldn't be so sure. I convinced Captain Denmark to leave a pulse relay satellite in Bersch's orbit before she leaves."

"Meaning?"

"Meaning that full power can be restored to the *Sentinel*, meaning that the technology and information of the Caretakers is at your fingertips, meaning you and your people can watch over this world as you were always meant to."

Bip's face froze in shock. "I don't know what to say..."

Handen grinned. "Light up a cigar, kid. Your adventure's only just begun."

With that, the former Hostilities Advisor keyed a few coordinates into the Do-fer, which began to whir its characteristic whir, then he stepped back to a safe distance.

"And I suppose you could say the same for me. Goodbye, Bip. It's been a...well, it's been interesting, I'll say that for sure."

Bip felt a tear trickle down his cheek. "Goodbye, Handen. I'll never forget you."

Handen threw a casual salute as the world began to wobble around him, then he disappeared.

Bip sat alone under a sky polka-dotted with a billion worlds. His quest was over, but his life was just beginning. He raised his mug and toasted the stars, which twinkled and winked knowingly in return. Then he went back to the party.

THE END…or is it?

If you enjoyed this book and would like to be notified of new releases, appearances, and everything else related to Steve Wetherell, sign up for the newsletter here -
http://eepurl.com/cv5FSj

Epilogue

What happened next?

Let's not say Happily Ever After. Nothing ends so simply, and people's lives would be incredibly unproductive if they just went around being happy all the time...

Needless to say, with the silver light in the sky gone and the world-threatening disaster that had united Bersch in fear and awe avoided, people went back to being people, as people are wont to do. The world continued to spin, as did the solar system and the galaxy and the universes and so on. And somewhere up above, a God did its job, and a red-faced man with metal teeth tried to make things difficult for people. And even above that, a gardener kept a close eye on his garden, checking all was as it should be.

And what of our heroes? What happened to them? Well, they got on with things...

Professor Riley DeChambre became a leading member of the parliament that filled the vacuum of Imperial rule, and Argustin's industry thrived as it had always done. Wars were fought as the world wriggled in a newfound freedom from Imperial oppression, but these too settled down eventually, as countries, tribes, and peoples found new oppressions to occupy their time.

As she said she would, Xharon returned home to look after her father, spending much of her time reminding a man with high things on his mind that eating and sleeping were important, nay necessary, for a healthy lifestyle. The pressures of her family's newfound political importance meant she became known merely as a princess rather than a warrior princess, which meant a lot of attending balls and laughing at bad jokes and generally being diplomatic to people she found boring. Though when she was alone, she would still twirl her axes at imaginary foes, and she kept her leather outfits oiled and ready, just in case.

Azron returned to the Free Countries, where he was hailed as a hero thief—even offered a chair on the board of the Port Town Union of Dodgy Fellows, and the prestigious rank of Solid Platinum Bloke. He turned it down, though, in favor of traveling to new and exciting places, where he could find new and exciting people to rob and new and exciting things to steal.

As for Handen...well, we can only guess at the stories of a man who is a lightning rod for trouble in a universe of endless possibilities. It's likely that his legend fills a library somewhere. More likely still that even in your world or your culture, there are ancient tales of a sword-wielding swashbuckler who appeared from nowhere to triumph in a time of crisis, and then afterward was never seen again.

And Bip? Bip did the right thing. In fact, he became renowned for doing the right thing because when someone says that you have to look after the entire world, it has a way of sharpening your sense of responsibility. And maybe, possibly, Bersch slept a little safer knowing that a fairly blameless guy who tried to do the right thing was looking out for it.

And the grand design? Well, it wouldn't be so grand if it could be spelled out, would it? And until you understand just how big the universes are, it's probably not a good idea to go poking around trying to sort out a Universal Theory.

What is the course of a raindrop through a river? Whichever way the river tells it. Which may or may not be backward.

Not enough? Well, maybe one day you'll meet an old man with wiry gray hair, who might just show you the world in the face of a painting. And maybe you'll see order, or maybe you'll see chaos. It just depends where you're standing, really...

*** THE END ***

Acknowledgments

Special thanks to Rebecca Hill for editing the initial publication of this book, and to Graham White for the original cover art.

About the Author

Steve Wetherell is an author, comedy writer and podcast idiot. He regularly writes humorous nonsense on the internet, and cordially invites you to join him. He lives in the English midlands with his wife, kids, and laptop, and his interests include beer, rock music and writing about himself in the third person.

Also by Steve Wetherell

Authors & Dragons - Podcast

Hell's Titties

The Totally Legend of Brandon Thighmaster

The Ballad of Aaron Bezron

Shoot the Dead

Far into the Dark

The Torso Farmer

Falstaff Books

**Want to know what's new
And coming soon from
Falstaff Books?**

Try This Free Ebook Sampler

https://www.instafreebie.com/free/bsZnl

**Follow the link.
Download the file.
Transfer to your e-reader, phone, tablet, watch, computer,
whatever.
Enjoy.**